"HURTS, DOESN'T IT?" SPIKE TAUNTED.

The Judge's hand was splayed over Angel's chest. Dru looked on, fascinated, thrilled, getting on her hands and knees like a lioness.

"Well, you know, it kind of itches a little," Angel tossed off, wincing. But nothing else happened. Dru kept waiting for the immolation.

Her Spike was angry. "Don't just stand there. Burn him!"

Angel made a face. He was obviously enjoying himself. "Gee, maybe he's broken."

"What the hell is going on?" Spike demanded.

Dru got it. She *knew*.

"There is no humanity in him." The Judge turned away, losing interest.

"Angel," Dru breathed, awash in delirious joy.

Angel grinned at her. Looked deep into her eyes with a sinister, wonderful gleam. They were connecting right here, and right now, and she could barely contain herself.

"Yeah, baby," he said, "I'm back."

Buffy the Vampire Slayer™

Buffy the Vampire Slayer (movie tie-in)
The Harvest
Halloween Rain
Coyote Moon
Night of the Living Rerun
The Angel Chronicles, Vol. 1
Blooded
The Angel Chronicles, Vol. 2
The Xander Years, Vol. 1
Visitors
Unnatural Selection
The Angel Chronicles, Vol. 3

Available from ARCHWAY Paperbacks

Buffy the Vampire Slayer adult books

Child of the Hunt
Return to Chaos
The Gatekeeper Trilogy
    Book 1: Out of the Madhouse
    Book 2: Ghost Roads
    Book 3: Sons of Entropy

The Watcher's Guide: The Official Companion to the Hit Show
The Postcards
The Essential Angel

Available from POCKET BOOKS

BUFFY
THE VAMPIRE
SLAYER™

THE ANGEL CHRONICLES
Vol. 3

A novelization by Nancy Holder
Based on the hit TV series created by Joss Whedon
Based on the teleplays "Surprise" by Marti Noxon,
"Innocence" by Joss Whedon
and "Passion" by Ty King

AN ARCHWAY PAPERBACK
Published by POCKET BOOKS
New York London Toronto Sydney Tokyo Singapore

AN ARCHWAY PAPERBACK *Original*

An Archway Paperback published by
POCKET BOOKS, a division of Simon & Schuster Inc.
1230 Avenue of the Americas, New York, NY 10020

™ and copyright © 1999 by Twentieth Century Fox Film Corporation.
All rights reserved.

All rights reserved, including the right to reproduce
this book or portions thereof in any form whatsoever.
For information address Pocket Books, 1230 Avenue
of the Americas, New York, NY 10020

ISBN: 0-671-02631-3

First Archway Paperback printing August 1999

10 9 8 7 6 5 4 3 2 1

AN ARCHWAY PAPERBACK and colophon are
registered trademarks of Simon & Schuster Inc.

Printed in the U.S.A.

IL 7+

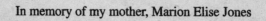

In memory of my mother, Marion Elise Jones

Acknowledgments

My deepest thanks to the cast and crew of *Buffy*, especially Joss Whedon, Marti Noxon, Ty King, and Caroline Kallas. Thanks, also, to Debbie Olshan at Fox. As always, my gratitude to my agent, Howard Morhaim, and his assistant Lindsay Sagnette; to my editor, Lisa Clancy, and assistant editor Liz Shiflett. *Todah rabah*, Michael Mantell, Ph.D.; Rabbi Zelig Plisken; and my Babysitter Battalion: Ida Khabazian, Julie Cross, Bekah and Julie Simpson, Lara and April Koljonen. Thanks also to my wonderful usual suspects—Charlie and Kathy Grant, Chris Golden, Leslie Jones, Karen Hackett, and Stinne Lighthart. Thank you also to Chris Mauricio and the Bronzers, for all their help and support. And last, but certainly not least, to my dear husband, Wayne, and our miraculous daughter, Belle . . . *we're on our way.*

THE CHRONICLES:

PROLOGUE

It was the dead of night.

Hands in the pockets of his black duster, Angel walked the moon-drenched streets of Sunnydale. His shadow loomed long, and his boot heels were the only sound above the night wind.

Like Angel himself, Sunnydale was cursed. Behind the pastel facades of its houses and the superficial, Southern California pleasantness of its population, terrible things happened as a matter of course. An astonishing number of people died, and in mind-numbingly brutal and savage ways. Children became possessed; babies became vampires. The dead not only walked, they raged.

The place had been known to the Spanish who'd founded it as Boca del Inferno, the mouth of hell. Sunnydale sucked evil in, exhaled it, vomited it. Its appetite for darkness was insatiable.

But evil also died here. Its executioner was Buffy Summers, the Slayer, the one girl chosen from all her generation to fight the demons, vampires, and monsters who long to corrupt and cripple the world. Buffy was a champion, a beacon, and a tragic hero of epic proportions: her battle was to the death ... hers. Slayers seldom lived long. Their lives were fierce and intense. And then they were over.

Angel's face was cast in shadow as he stopped before the yellow house on Revello Drive. As the moonlight made hollows of his eyes and cheeks, he stared up at the bedroom where Buffy lay sleeping. Mind and body— yes, and soul—pulsed like a heartbeat with thoughts of her. He was restless and edgy, and he could admit now, in the darkness, that it was his need for her that had driven him out of his apartment to stand here, now.

The ultimate irony in all of this was, of course, that Angel was a vampire, in love with a vampire slayer. Not just any vampire; in his heyday he had been known as Angelus, the One with the Angelic Face. No other vampire could match him in sheer cruelty and unbelievable brutality.

Though he still looked like the reckless young Irishman he once had been, he was over two hundred years old. He was also the only vampire on earth with a soul, tormented by the horrors he had committed after he had been changed.

In Galway, in 1753, his schoolmaster had seen a rogue and a scoundrel. Angel's father had seen a callow lad who spent his time at the faro tables with bad friends and worse women. Only Darla, the exquisite vampire who had sired him, had sensed the passion in him. The need to live a larger life. The drive to see, and do, and be something other than an Irish gentleman in a provincial town.

How had she known? No mirror could tell Angel what she had seen. Perhaps it had been the hunger in his eyes. The crooked but eager smile when he had approached her. The crack in his voice when he had confessed his longing to see the world.

Darla had known much about longing. About passion.

But Buffy Summers *was* Angel's passion.

She's just a girl, he reminded himself. She would turn seventeen in two days.

But she was also the Slayer. Nightly she faced mortal combat; every morning when she awoke, she knew it might be her last day on earth. As did he. That changed everything.

Or is that how I excuse the fact that I can't stay away from her?

THE FIRST CHRONICLE:

Surprise

PROLOGUE

In her sleep, Buffy Summers stirred. She opened her eyes, registering the stillness, and turned on the light, crowned with an upside-down lampshade, on her nightstand. She took a drink of water and slowly got out of bed.

Then she padded down the hall to the bathroom in her blue satin pajamas and black tank top . . .

Ah, there she is, Drusilla thought, as she stepped behind the Slayer and followed her down the hall. Drusilla, the beautiful mad vampire who had been sired by Angelus, hated the Slayer beyond all reason. On so many levels, the girl was a threat: not only to life and limb, but to her unbeating heart. Angelus—now called Angel—loved this human girl, when he should be panting around Dru like a starving dog. Because of Buffy, he had joined the white hats against his own kind. He murdered vampires; he crept up and staked them without warning. He eliminated helpful demons.

Worst of all, with Buffy and another Slayer named Kendra, he had seriously injured Dru's other true love, Spike, in his attempt to restore Dru's health. Granted, the ritual had required sacrificing Angel, but when a guy loved a girl—really loved her—he would do anything for her, wouldn't he? Spike was all about pleasing her. But thanks to Buffy, Angel was all about killing her.

Drusilla would not rest until those who would harm her and Spike were destroyed. She had already slashed Kendra's throat—and it had been marvelous. When she found the proper moment, she would kill Angel as well. And Buffy . . . Blood pooled in the corners of Drusilla's mouth, a nice contrast to her black gown, as she silently followed Buffy through her house.

Buffy, I shall kill tonight. As soon as I can.

Sleepily, Buffy opened the door to the bathroom, and inexplicably stepped into the Bronze, the club where everyone in Sunnydale hooked up.

Though there was no band, music echoed hauntingly off the walls as smiling couples glided together. Their smiles were dreamy; they moved slowly, passing around and beneath glows of golden light and into shadow. Making her way through what seemed a maze of languid, otherworldly images, Buffy was dazed. She felt as though she were underwater, and yet, she was part of the otherworldly scene, so she didn't quite make sense, either.

Her redheaded best friend, Willow Rosenberg, perched at one of the Bronze's high, round tables. A large cup of coffee steamed on a saucer, and an organ grinder's monkey in a little red cap and jacket chittered beside Willow on the table. Very matter-of-factly, Willow told Buffy, in French, "The hippo stole his pants." Then she smiled perkily and waved at Buffy. Buffy waved uncertainly back.

Bewildered, she walked on, to come upon her mother, standing by a post and drinking coffee from a cup very much like Willow's. As she lifted the cup to her lips, she regarded Buffy eerily and asked her daughter, "Do you really think you're ready, Buffy?"

Buffy frowned. "What?"

As Buffy waited for a response, the saucer slipped from Joyce's grasp, crashed to the floor, and shattered. As if she didn't even notice, Joyce blankly turned and walked dreamily away.

Again, Buffy moved on, finding herself on the dance floor. Couples danced, the whispery, sensuous music twining around them, as Buffy wandered, alone.

Then the crowd parted.

And like a candle in the darkness, he was there.

Angel, she thought radiantly, as the tall, mysterious vampire smiled back at her. Dressed all in black, he was the center of the room; there was light in his face—for her—and light in her heart, as their eyes met and held. Though he stood several feet away, she felt his touch on her skin, the brush of his lips on her cheek. His smoldering gaze told her he felt the same; no one could love this much, and want this much, and not feel it . . .

As if in a trance, they walked toward each other, hands outstretched.

Oh, my love, Buffy thought. *My life . . .*

Then like an attacking beast, Drusilla appeared behind Angel. As Buffy watched in horror, the vampire raised a large, gleaming knife and stabbed him viciously in the back.

Buffy screamed, "Angel!"

His shaking hand strained toward hers, crumbling to ashes before her eyes. He had time to look at her, with a soft moan, and agony in his eyes—*Buffy, help me; love me forever . . .*

He exploded into dust.

Drusilla stood fully revealed in her true vampire face, her golden eyes shining with glee.

"Happy Birthday, Buffy," she said, relishing Buffy's despair.

Buffy bolted upright, panting and sickened with terror.

She was in her bed.

It had been a dream.

Nothing but a dream.

CHAPTER 1

Since moving to Sunnydale, Angel had lived in a sub-basement apartment. He kept the lights muted, favoring Japanese-style lamps of paper, and decorated the apartment with only a few prized possessions from his many years of life. It was a lonely place in many ways, but it was his sanctuary as well. In life, he had not been much of an intellectual. But that was one thing he had remedied since becoming a vampire. In fact, he thought too much. And too much thinking led to brooding.

There was a soft knock at his door. It was just past dawn, and he had been fast asleep. Like his evil vampire brethren, Angel slept during the day, if he slept at all.

Muzzily, he got out of bed in his drawstring sweats and moved to answer the door.

"Angel?" Buffy called through the door.

The sound of her voice both delighted and puzzled him. He was unused to seeing her during the day.

"Hold on," he told her, opening the door.

She was beautiful, dressed for school in a very short black-and-white dress and a white jacket. He was very aware of the fact that he was half-dressed as he stepped back to let her in.

"Hey, I . . . everything okay?" he asked her, his protective concern for her at least temporarily replacing his instantaneous reaction of lust upon smelling her vanilla perfume and sweeping his gaze over her lovely body.

She gazed up at him, searching his face. Her face was clouded with worry. "That's what I was going to ask you. You're okay, right?"

He was thrown by the alarm in her voice. "Sure. I'm fine. What's up?"

She walked in and set down her purse, looking away. She wiped her mouth and looped her hair around her ear, gestures she made when she was nervous or uneasy. "I had this dream that Drusilla was alive."

Drusilla, he thought. The last time he had seen her, she had nearly killed him. In his remorse for what he had done to her, he had almost welcomed the torture she had inflicted on him, splashing him with holy water so that his flesh burned and blistered.

When he had met her back in England during the Victorian era, she had been an innocent young girl tormented by her ability to see visions. Angel had used her fear against her and driven her insane. But first, he killed everyone she loved—all her family and her friends. When she tried to escape him by entering a convent, he changed her into a vampire the same night she took her holy vows.

He was her sire, as Darla had been his. He had made her what she was. And he, Buffy, and Kendra had destroyed her. Of that he was certain.

But Buffy was clearly upset. Angel asked softly, "What happened?" In a gesture of good manners, and not from any desire on his part to do so, he moved to put on his shirt as he waited for her answer.

Buffy spoke in a rush, looking up at him as if to reassure herself that he was still there. "She killed you. Right in front of me."

"It was just a dream," he soothed, longing to comfort her in his embrace. "It wasn't real."

"It felt so real." Her voice was raspy and frightened. Her eyes were huge in her delicate face.

He tried to satisfy his need to hold her by cupping her cheek. "It wasn't. I'm right here."

She moved her face into his hand, then took a breath and rushed on. Tingles raced through his body. With all the focus he could muster, he tried to concentrate on her words.

"Angel, this happened before. The dreams that I had about the Master. They came true."

The Master—who had once been *his* master—had been an evil vampire king trapped in a ruined church beneath Sunnydale. Buffy had dreamed of him before he made his presence known. The Master had succeeded in actually killing Buffy. Xander Harris, a guy friend of Buffy's who loved her and detested Angel, had brought her back to life with CPR. Angel could not have done it;

he had no breath in his lungs to give her. If Xander had not been there, Buffy would be dead now.

Exactly as she dreamed.

"Still," he said now, trying to calm himself as well as Buffy, as he touched the lapel of her jacket, "not every dream you have comes true. I mean, what else did you dream last night?" He kept his voice gentle. "Can you remember?"

She thought a moment. Then she looked a little sheepish.

"I dreamed that Giles and I opened an office supply warehouse in Vegas."

He smiled. "You see my point."

"Yeah. I do." She looked down, then back up at him. "But what if Drusilla is alive? I mean, we never saw her body."

He embraced her gently to stop the torrent of words, and of her fear. *If Drusilla's alive, she won't rest until Buffy's dead. And I can never permit that.*

"She's not." His voice was firm and he looked at her steadily, though his own alarm was growing. "But even if she was, we'd deal."

Buffy was not placated. "But what if she—"

This time, he silenced her with a kiss. She tensed for a second, and then she relaxed into it. Her lips were hot against his cool mouth; her body was strong and coursing with energy. The room was charged; the intensity rose in the dark intimacy of his apartment.

The bed, he thought, *I'll carry her there, and—*

No.

With extreme difficulty, he finished the kiss, pulling

gently away, though inside he was on fire. "What if what?"

Her voice was a whisper, as she said, "I'm sorry. Were we talking?"

Oh, Buffy. Sweet Buffy.

Who began the next kiss? They moved as one being; when their lips touched, they both gasped. Arms reached, caressed, embraced; rings glinted as fingers gripped arms and shoulders, caressed necks, and caught up handfuls of hair. The kiss grew; was it another kiss or the same one?

Is there a world anywhere but here, in her arms?

She leaned up and into him; he was bowed slightly over her, wanting her desperately, his passion rising. He lost track of thought; all he was, was need.

And then she broke away, looking a little frightened, and stammered, "I'm sorry, I . . . I have to go to school."

She turned and almost ran, and though he said, "I know," he followed her, grabbed her arm, and pulled her around into his embrace.

They were kissing again, as they were meant to. He wanted her so much. He needed her.

"Oh, God, you feel—" she whispered.

In that moment, he knew he had a choice to make. He chose for her, not for himself.

He said, "You have to go to school."

She began to walk backward toward the door. "All right. This is me. I'm going."

Her gaze said otherwise. He pursued her. He couldn't stop himself. Lover, predator—he was both. Vampires did not ask for things. They did not deny themselves.

They took.

He came up to her and put his arms around her. The door was a welcome barrier to her flight as her back pushed against it. She raised her right hand slightly and it fluttered down onto his shoulder as she moaned. He kept kissing her, allowing himself to reveal how much he wanted her, his need growing, as he neared her neck with his kisses. He almost bit down. She gave a tiny cry, perhaps not realizing what she was doing, and then they both smiled a little. He was, after all, a vampire. Danger was mixed in with the lust, and the love.

Too much danger, Angel told himself, *for her. Slayer she might be, but she's very young, and still innocent. It's up to me to be strong.*

She would never realize what it took for him to break the mood as he said, "You still haven't told me what you want for your birthday."

She smiled sweetly at him, looking girlish and a little shy, and said, "Surprise me."

"Okay."

This kiss was the last for now; they both knew it, and there was a calm finality to it that allowed Angel to savor it without worrying about going too far again.

"This is nice," Buffy murmured, more at ease now. "I like seeing you first thing in the morning."

"It's bedtime for me," Angel reminded her.

"Then I like seeing you at bedtime," she countered. She blinked, as if she realized how that sounded. And again, she was a young girl, blushing and stammering, "I—you know what I mean . . ."

He took it upon himself to smooth over the situation. "I think so." Then he realized he was not that noble. "What do you mean?"

"That I like seeing you." Her face lost all shyness, if not its heartbreaking sweetness. "And the part at the end of the night where we say goodbye, it's getting harder."

Angel looked deep into her eyes. "Yeah," he admitted. "It is."

They gazed at each other. Neither spoke again.

They were both too afraid to.

Willow could not contain her amazement. She stared wide-eyed at her best friend, her eyebrows hidden by her large purplish-blue felt hat as they walked toward school.

" 'I like seeing you at bedtime?' You actually *said* that?"

Buffy shrugged, but she was embarrassed and excited and well, a little proud, too. Her cheeks were very warm. "I know. I know."

Willow wasn't finished. "Man. That's like . . . I don't know. That's moxie or something!"

"Totally unplanned," Buffy assured her with a wave of her hand. "It just came out."

"And he was into it?" Willow persisted. "He wants to see you at bedtime, too?"

"Yeah," Buffy said. "I think he does. I mean, he's cool about it."

"Well, of course he is," Willow said brightly. " 'Cause he's cool. He would never, you know—"

"Push," Buffy finished for her.

Willow nodded. "Right. He's not the type."

Loyal Willow. Buffy was so glad she had someone she could really talk to.

"Willow, what am I going to do?"

"What do you want to do?" Willow asked back.

"I don't know," Buffy answered, trying to be honest. It would be easy to pretend she was so virtuous that she wasn't even considering her options. But Willow wouldn't judge her; of that she was certain.

The two sat down at the same time and faced each other. "I mean, *want* isn't always the right thing to do. To act on want can be wrong."

Willow considered. "True."

"But to not act on want." Buffy frowned at the thought of never being with Angel, *really* being with him. Her life was not the same as other girls'. Didn't that mean some of the rules were different, too? "What if I never feel this way again?" *What if I die without knowing love?*

Willow smiled. "*Carpe diem.* You told me that once."

Buffy was bewildered. "Fish of the day?"

Willow's smile grew into a chuckle. "Not carp. *Carpe.* It means 'seize the day.' "

"Right." Buffy hesitated. Her heart was racing. Her entire being sang as she realized she had made her decision.

"I think we're going to," she admitted finally. "To seize it. Once you get to a certain point, then seizing is sort of inevitable."

She looked for Willow's reaction—shock? disapproval?—but as she had anticipated, Willow was clearly on her side.

"Wow," she said, a bit wistfully, obviously very impressed.

Buffy smiled, feeling a little shy, a little excited, and very relieved. "Yeah."

"Wow," Willow repeated, in the same awed tone.

The school bell rang. Buffy groaned and stood up. Willow did the same, trailing after her.

"Wow," she said again

She caught up with Buffy.

"Wow."

Buffy said, more happily, "Yeah." Then she glanced over at the concrete picnic tables—more specifically, at a guy sitting on top of one of them, strumming an electric guitar. A large black amp sat beside him on the table. *Now it's Willow's turn to think a few things through.*

"Hey," Buffy drawled coyly, "speaking of wow potential, there's Oz over there. What are we thinking? Any sparkage?"

Willow glowed. "He's nice. I like his hands."

Buffy was delighted. "Ooh, fixing on insignificant details is a definite crush sign."

"I don't know, though," Willow added humbly. "I mean, he *is* a senior."

Buffy was unimpressed, although, in theory, she understood Willow's hesitation. "You think he's too old 'cause he's a senior? Please. My boyfriend had a bicentennial."

Willow's voice rose. "That's true." Then she began to lose her nerve again. "I guess . . . I just . . ."

Buffy sensed it was time to push. Willow was so good. *She deserves a nice boyfriend to go out with and have fun with. Okay, he doesn't know about my secret Clark Kent identity and all the rest of that—he's not a Slayerette, as Xander would say, but we'll figure out how to keep him out of the loop without making it weird. And speaking of old, unrequited loves . . .*

"You can't spend the rest of your life waiting for Xander to wake up and smell the hottie. Make a move," she prodded. "Do the talking thing."

Willow was not thoroughly convinced. "What if the talking thing becomes the awkward silence thing?"

"Well, you won't know unless you try," Buffy reminded her. Then she moved on ahead, leaving Willow to do just that.

Gulp.

Willow gathered her courage and walked up behind Oz. He was still sitting on the picnic table, strumming his guitar.

"Hey," she said, coming around to his side.

As soon as he heard her voice, he stopped strumming and looked up at her. "Hey," he said back, giving her his full attention. That was one of the things she really liked about him. He knew that listening was more than waiting for your turn to talk.

But here it was her turn to talk again, already! *Which I know how to do,* she reminded herself firmly.

"Do you guys, uh, have a gig tonight?" she asked, aiming for hip, knowing she was falling oh-so short.

"No. Practice," he answered. "See, our band's kind of

moving toward this new sound . . . where we suck. So, practice."

"I think you guys sound good," she said, smiling. *I'm talking to him. Even better, we're talking to each other.*

"Thanks," he replied, looking genuinely complimented.

Suddenly she felt a little shyer. "I bet you have a lot of groupies."

A smile flickered over his features, flattered and touched. "It happens. But I'm living groupie-free nowadays," he assured her. "I'm clean."

"Oh." As he looked down at his guitar, she bit her lip. She was running out of steam. *Argh. Time for the awkward silence thing.*

Then he gazed at her and said, "I'm going to ask you to go out with me tomorrow night, and I'm kind of nervous about it, actually. It's interesting."

Wow. She reeled. *Wow.*

"Well, if it helps at all," she breathed, "I'm going to say yes."

Oz nodded seriously. "Yeah, it helps. It creates a comfort zone." His smile returned. "Do you want to go out with me tomorrow night?"

Willow winced and clapped her forehead through her hat. "Oh, I can't!" *Tragedy! Frustration!*

Oz appeared unfazed. "Oh, see, I like that you're unpredictable."

And unbelievably bad timing. "It's just that it's Buffy's birthday and we're throwing her a surprise party."

He was still unfazed. "It's okay."

"But you could come," she realized. "If you wanted." Giving him an out.

He hesitated. "Well, I don't want to crash."

"No, it's fine," she urged. "You could be my . . . date."

Oz smiled his Oz smile again, warm and slightly amused and very charming. "All right. I'm in."

She kind of lost it there for a moment. This had never happened to her before. She made as if to leave; he lowered his head as if to show that he understood that she needed to get going. Breathlessly, grinning, she walked away, murmuring to herself, "I said 'date.' "

Wow.

Cordelia had a lot to do, including remembering her new copy of *Allure* to read during study hall. As she fished it out of her locker, Xander Harris stood closely behind her, trying to look like he wasn't hanging around.

"So. Buffy's party," he ventured. *"Mañana."*

She was a little irritated by the interruption, more so by where he might be going with that opener, so she said, "Well, just because she's Miss 'Save the World' we have to make a big deal. I have to cook." She faced him. "And everything."

"You're cooking?" Xander repeated carefully, as if he couldn't quite believe his ears. She heard the mockery in his tone.

"Well, I'm chips and dips girl," she announced, feeling a little defensive.

"Horrors," he teased. "All that opening and stirring."

"And shopping and carrying," she reminded him, not letting him get to her. *At all.*

"Well, you should have a person who does such things for you."

"That's what I've been saying to my father," she said, returning to the serious business of going through her locker. "But does he listen?"

Xander was still not going away. He leaned in toward her and said, "So. You're going. And I'm going. Should we—maybe—go?"

"Why?" she asked in utter astonishment, even though of course by now, she wasn't astonished. *When you're a veteran dater like me, you rarely get ambushed.*

Xander shrugged. "I don't know. This thing with us? Despite our better judgment, it keeps happening. Maybe we should just admit that we're dating—"

Oh, yeah, right. Xander Harris and Cordelia Chase, an official couple. As if.

"Groping in a broom closet is not dating," she informed him. "You don't call it a date until the guy spends money."

"Fine. I'll spend. Then we'll grope." He was all intensity and she was not loving it. Guys who wanted to be with her were usually much suaver about the whole deal. *For one thing, they don't make fun of me most of the time they're around me.*

He must have gotten the message. "Whatever. I just think it's just some kind of a whack that we have to hide it from all our friends."

She got in his face. "Well, of course you want to tell everybody. You have nothing to be ashamed of. I, on the other hand, have everything to be ashamed of."

Xander blinked. "You know what? 'Nuff said. Forget

it. It must have been my multiple personality guy talking. I call him Idiot Jed, glutton for punishment."

He huffed at her and walked off.

Good, she thought. *Thank God. Fine.*

But way down deep, she was a little impressed with him for standing up to her. Not that she would ever admit it. Not to anyone, especially herself.

Rupert Giles, officially in America as the librarian of the Sunnydale High School library, was walking through the school lounge with his briefcase and a few copies of some archeology magazines when he caught sight of Buffy's good friend, Xander.

Giles was Buffy's Watcher, the person charged with mentoring her and training her in her capacity as Slayer. Part drill instructor, part guidance counselor, and, in his case, a friend, though the Watchers' Council frowned on that sort of thing. The Watcher's job required that he or she be willing and able to send the Slayer to her death, if that was what was necessary to win a battle—not the war; that had been going on for centuries—between good and evil.

The war would continue on, long after he and Buffy both were dust.

But these morose thoughts were the furthest things from his mind as he greeted Xander.

"Good morning," Giles said pleasantly. "Everything in order for the party?"

"Absolutely," Xander replied, but he seemed a little downhearted. "Ready to get down, you funky party weasel?"

Just then, Giles spied Buffy and Miss Calendar coming down the stairs. Jenny Calendar was a wonder to him—young, lovely, clever, and a "technopagan," of all things. She had instantly grasped Buffy's role in the scheme of things here on the Hellmouth without so much as a blink. And Giles's role, as well. Twice now, she had pushed her sleeves up—figuratively speaking—and pitched in to thwart the forces of darkness.

As she and Buffy drew near, Giles leaned toward Xander and whispered. "Ah. Here comes Buffy. Remember—discretion is the better part of valor."

"You could have just gone, *ssh*," Xander shot back. "God, are all you Brits such drama queens?"

Buffy and Miss Calendar came up beside them. The young man shifted his attention and said, in a sweetly teasing voice, "Buffy, I feel a pre-birthday spanking coming on." He rubbed his hands together in mock anticipation.

Buffy gave him a look that would melt steel as Miss Calendar said, "I'd curb that impulse if I were you, Xander."

"Check," he said, pretending to talk into a lapel microphone. "Cancel spanking."

Buffy and Miss Calendar sat at a round table. Giles and Xander joined them. Giles frowned gently at Buffy. She looked pale and drawn.

"Are you all right, Buffy? You seem a little fatigued."

"Rough night," she admitted. "I had a dream that Drusilla was alive. And she killed Angel." She made a face, as if even saying the words upset her. "It just really freaked me out."

Giles moved into Watcher mode without even thinking

about it. After all his time in the role, what had once felt awkward and artificial was what he now considered to be "the real Giles."

"So you feel it was more of a portent," he observed, picking his words carefully.

She moved her shoulders as she sighed. "See, I don't know. I don't want to start a big freak-out over nothing—"

"Still. Best to be on the alert. If Drusilla is alive, it could be fairly cataclysmic."

And that's putting it mildly, he thought. *Were she alive, her singular goal—her mission, as it were—would be to avenge herself against my Slayer.*

"Again," Xander reproved, "so many words. Couldn't you just say we'd be in trouble?"

Giles had painfully learned the value of patience, through his dealings with Xander, and he mentally thanked him again for another small lesson as he said tiredly, "Go to class, Xander."

"Gone." Xander stood and turned to leave. Then he looked back at the group. "Notice the economy of phrasing. 'Gone.' Simple. Direct."

And he made himself gone.

Buffy rose from of her chair. "Maybe I should get gone, too."

Giles also stood. Attempting to act unconcerned, he said, "Don't worry yourself unduly, Buffy. I'm sure it's nothing."

"I know." She tried to look less nervous. "I should keep my Slayer cool. But it's Angel, which automatically equals maxi-wig."

Giles smiled at her as she left to start her day as a high school student.

But his day as a Watcher had already begun, and as he stood there, his smile fading, he sincerely hoped Buffy's dream meant nothing.

Yet I cannot be certain of that, not at all. And God help us if that monster is alive. God help us all.

Dalton, the shy but loyal vampire scribe, arrived at the factory and stepped into the expansive, candlelit room with the iron box in his arms. His previous leader, the young boy called the Anointed One, had brought the local vampires to this lair after the Master died. When they had followed the Master, they had dwelled underground. The Master had been mystically imprisoned inside a sunken church. Those days were long gone, as were the days of the Anointed One.

He called into the shadows, "I have your package."

A familiar voice replied imperiously, if wearily, "Just put it on the table. Near the other gifts."

Looking weary, Dalton's boss, Spike, rolled his wheelchair into view. It was Spike who had destroyed the Anointed One, grabbing him off his seat of honor and imprisoning him in a cage, then hoisting the cage through the factory roof and into the sunlight. The small but immensely powerful vampire had burned to ash.

Now Spike, too, had been burned. While trying to restore Drusilla to health in an old Sunnydale church, he had been attacked by two Slayers and that turncoat, Angel. And a handful of humans, but Dalton mentally dismissed them. People were for eating, and not much else.

Spike was deathly pale, and scarred from the fire. It was a miracle he was still alive—a testament to his strength.

As Dalton moved to obey him, he caught sight of Drusilla walking up behind the wheelchair, healthy and vibrant, dressed in a tight red sleeveless dress. Spike's sacrifices had not been in vain: he had succeeding in curing his beloved, and now their roles were reversed. It was Drusilla who took care of Spike.

"Are you dead set on this, pet?" Spike asked Drusilla in a world-weary tone. "Wouldn't you rather have your party in Vienna?"

Trying not to eavesdrop, Dalton put his box next to two similar boxes. Two other vampires were decorating for the party, one twining red flowers into the backs of tall wooden chairs.

Pouty, Drusilla said, "But the invitations are sent."

Spike looked more frustrated than anything. He would never deny Drusilla anything she really wanted. Although sometimes it was admittedly difficult to figure out what was a fleeting whim of hers and what she was serious about having.

"Yeah, but, it's just, I've had it with this place. Nothing ever comes off the way it's supposed to."

Truer words were never spoken, Dalton thought glumly. His boss looked terrible. Strong and vigorous before the battle in the church with the Slayers, now he was stuck in a wheelchair.

Drusilla lovingly put her arms around Spike and said,

"My gatherings are always perfect. Remember Spain, Spike?" With a huge, knowing smile on her face, she crouched down beside him and walked her fingers seductively up his thighs and chest. "The bulls?" The look she gave him was filled with secrets—and promises—meant only for him.

Finally a smile flashed across Spike's face. "I remember, sweet." The smile faded. "But Sunnydale is cursed for us. Angel and the Slayer see to that."

"Ssh," she breathed into his ear. "I've got good games for everyone." Adoringly, she licked the scars on the side of his face. "You'll see." Then she left him, smiling radiantly, to survey the work on the flowers.

Her face fell. She began to shake. "These flowers are wrong. They're all wrong." She moaned. "I can't abide them!"

She started ripping them out, losing control, her face contorting with rage and horror. As instantly as she had started, she stopped, bringing a trembling hand to her face.

Spike looked tiredly at the two vamps. "Let's try something different with the flowers, then," he said, with the voice of someone who had gone through this kind of thing many times before.

Then Drusilla's mood changed yet again. Glowing with good-nature, she advanced on the table of presents with wide, girlish eyes.

"Can I open one?" She grinned coquettishly through her lashes at her lover. "Can I? Can I?"

Spike chuckled indulgently. "Just a peek, love. They're for the party."

Bouncing on her heels with excitement, she opened the very box that Dalton had just brought. She looked inside with rapturous glee.

"Do you like it baby?" Spike asked, obviously certain that she did. There was pride in his voice. He knew very well that he had pulled something off.

"It reeks of death," she said, immeasurably delighted. She went to Spike and knelt before him, stroking his knees and things. "This will be the best party ever."

"Why's that?" he asked warmly.

"Because," she said rising and turning back to the box, "it will be the last."

With the flourish of a very strong and very mad vampire, she slammed the box shut.

CHAPTER 2

In the sunny kitchen of the Summers' house on Revello Drive, Joyce was clearing the breakfast plates while Buffy looped on her stretchy wire bracelets. An open birthday card sat on the counter.

It was the morning of Buffy's seventeenth birthday. She felt refreshed and up. No bad dreams and a good night's sleep. She was having a birthday just like any other high school kid with the misfortune to be born on a school day.

"Mall trip for your birthday on Saturday," her mom reminded her. "Don't forget."

As if. Buffy gave her a look. "Space on a mom-sponsored shopping opportunity? Not likely."

"So," Joyce said, "does seventeen feel any different than sixteen?"

"It's funny you should ask that," Buffy replied cheerily. *I feel great.* "You know, I woke up feeling more mature, responsible, and level-headed."

Her mom knew she was up to something. "Really? It's uncanny."

Buffy nodded. "I now possess the qualities one looks for in a licensed driver." She was asking the big question, and her mom obviously got it.

Her mom frowned slightly. "Buffy—"

"You said we could talk about it again when I was seventeen," Buffy pointed out.

Joyce turned from the sink with a plate in her hands. "Do you really think you're ready, Buffy?" she asked, echoing the question she had asked in Buffy's nightmare.

Then the plate slipped from her hands and shattered on the floor.

Buffy stiffened in shock. She went numb from head to toe, as if she had been plunged in ice water.

It was the dream . . . coming true . . .

I wonder if I should change my clothes tonight before Buffy's party, Jenny Calendar thought idly, as she balanced her books, her purse, and a nice hot cup of herbal tea and carried them into her computer science classroom. She put her things down on the desk and starting organizing her papers for first period. *We'll cover Applets,* she thought. *These kids are ready for the big stuff . . .*

Behind her, someone said her name very slowly, in a thick Eastern European accent—"Jen-ny Calen-dar"—as if sounding it out for the first time.

She jumped and whirled around.

He had been reading her name off the blackboard. He was a tall man, wearing the clothes of the Old Country: a brown hat, a white shirt with a black lace tie, and a large silver pin on his vest.

He was no stranger to her, but she was uncomfortable in his presence nonetheless: he was her superior in their clan, both by blood and obligation. He was her Uncle Enyos.

And he looked extremely displeased with her.

"You startled me," she said, struggling to compose herself.

"You look well." There was an edge in his voice.

"Yes, I'm fine." *He's angry. I'm not surprised. I would be, too, if our places were switched. But then he would feel the same way I've come to feel.*

She walked briskly behind her desk. "I know I haven't written as much lately. I've been busy."

His displeasure grew. "I cannot imagine what is so important to make you ignore your responsibility to your people."

He's absolutely right. Nothing should be more important. Still, she tried to excuse herself. "I've been working, and—"

"The elder woman has been reading signs," he cut in. "Something is different."

"Nothing has changed," Jenny said firmly. "The curse still holds."

"The elder woman is never wrong," he countered. "She says his pain is lessening. She can feel it."

Oh, damn, Jenny thought. *I don't want to be a part of this any more.*

"There is . . ." She trailed off.

Her uncle leaned forward. "There is . . . what?"

"A girl," she said, with difficulty. She felt like the worst of betrayers. *Rupert, I'm sorry,* she thought, hoping he would never learn the truth about who she was and why she was in Sunnydale.

The old man's eyes filled with fire. "Oh, *what?*" he cried with disbelief. "How could you let this happen?"

"I promise you," she said, "Angel still suffers. And he makes amends for his evil. He even saved my life."

"So you just forget?" His voice rose in anger. "That he destroyed the most beloved daughter of your tribe? That he killed every man, woman, and child that touched her life?"

She looked down.

His voice thundered. "Vengeance demands that his pain be eternal, as ours is. If this—this *girl* gives him one minute of happiness, it is one minute too much."

She sighed heavily. "I'm sorry. I thought—"

"You thought what? You thought you are Jenny Calendar now? You are still Janna, of the Kalderash people. A Gypsy."

"I know," she said, her features hardening, no longer defensive. He had no idea what it had been like here, bonding with Buffy and her friends. He would be shocked at how torn she felt. "Uncle, *I know.*"

"Then prove it," he returned. "Your time for watching is past. The girl and him—it ends now. Do what you must to take her from him."

She kept her chin raised, but her face softened with sympathy for Buffy, and for Angel as well. A great sadness washed over her at the unfairness of what she now saw as a misguided attempt to right an ancient wrong.

"I will see to it." *And I will, even though nothing in me wants to.*

Not completely satisfied, but with nothing more to say, her uncle left.

She stood behind her desk, suddenly realizing the absurdity her life had become: Jenny Calendar, hip young technopagan, was in actuality a Gypsy spy, who was about to do whatever she could to break the Slayer's heart.

Buffy sat in the library with Giles, her stomach clenched with nerves. It was so hard to believe this was the same day she'd awakened to: the early morning so nice, and now everything so out of whack.

The typical, average day of a Slayer, even on her birthday.

"And then my mom broke the plate," she continued, telling him about her morning. "It was just like my dream. Every gesture. Every word. It was so creepy."

Giles considered thoughtfully. "Yes. I'd imagine it would be fairly unnerving."

He sat on the study table with his pastel-striped coffee mug in his left hand as Xander and Willow came bursting into the room.

"Hey," Xander called, "it's the woman of the hour."

Willow skipped over to Buffy to give her a big hug. "It's happy birthday Buffy!"

Willow must have sensed her mood, because she

backed off and raised her eyebrows. "Not happy birthday Buffy?"

Buffy glumly sat in her chair. Giles took over. "It's just that . . . a part of the nightmare Buffy had the other night actually transpired."

Even hearing him say it gave Buffy a wiggins.

"Which means Drusilla might still be alive," Buffy added, raising the wiggins bar a couple of extra notches. She turned to Giles for support. "Giles, in my dream, I couldn't stop her. She *blindsided* me. Angel was gone before I knew what happened."

Giles looked at her dead on. "Even if she is alive, we can still protect Angel. Dreams aren't prophecies, Buffy. You dreamed the Master had risen, but you stopped it from happening."

Angel said the same thing, she almost told Giles. *In his apartment yesterday morning, when we . . . when I wanted to stay. When I was mostly hoping he'd pick me up and carry me over to his—*

Xander nodded, crossing his arms over his chest. "You ground his bones to make your bread."

Somewhat comforted by Xander's firm, no-nonsense tone, Buffy relaxed a tiny bit. "That's true. Except for the bread part. Okay, so, fine. We're one step ahead." She gazed levelly at her Watcher. "I want to stay that way."

"Absolutely." Giles jumped into action. "Let me read up on Drusilla. See if she has any particular patterns. Why don't you meet me here at seven? We'll map out a strategy."

"What am I supposed to do until then?" she asked softly, feeling cast adrift.

He gestured with his mug as he walked into his office. "Go to classes, do you homework, have supper."

"Right," she murmured, standing and gathering up her white backpack and jacket. "Be *that* Buffy." The normal girl with the mundane existence. The birthday girl whose thoughts would be on the upcoming trip to the mall and wondering if she was going to get her driver's license after all.

Not the Slayer, whose vampire boyfriend might even, at this moment, be dead.

As she left the library, Xander said dispiritedly, "Well, *that's* not a perky birthday puppy."

Sounding just as bummed, Willow said, "So much for our surprise party. I bought little hats and everything."

"Mmm-hmm," Xander replied, sharing her disappointment.

"Oh, well. I'll tell Cordelia." Willow rolled her eyes in distaste.

Standing in the doorway to his office, Giles said, "No, you won't. We're having a party tonight."

Xander raised his brows and stared at Giles the way he had stared at the broken pots and spears at the Sunnydale Museum on their most recent field trip.

"Looks like Mr. Caution Man, but the sound he makes is funny," Xander riffed.

"Buffy's surprise party will go ahead as we've planned," Giles insisted. "Except I won't be wearing the little hat."

Willow scrunched up her face. "But Buffy and Angel—"

"May well be in danger," Giles cut in. "As they have been before, and I imagine, will be again. One thing I have learned in my tenure here on the Hellmouth is that there is never a good time to relax. But Buffy's turning seventeen just this once, and she deserves a party." *So few Slayers make it to seventeen*, he added mentally, but did not say.

Xander was impressed. "You're a great man of our time."

"And anyway, Angel's coming," Willow added, cheering up. "So she'll be able to protect him *and* have cake."

"Precisely," Giles concurred.

Pleased, Xander and Willow went off to do the school thing.

It had been a long day, especially for a birthday. When you don't have a lot of friends at school, not many people know it even *is* your birthday. Now the only special event on her birthday night would be her seven o'clock meeting with Giles.

As she walked down the empty corridor, Miss Calender stepped from the shadows. "Buffy," she said, as Buffy jumped, startled.

Buffy smoothed back her hair. "Oh, my God. I didn't see you there."

She liked Miss Calendar. She was smart and pretty, and it was obvious to one and all that she had the hots for Giles. Buffy was happy for him. Plus, Miss Calendar knew about the good-and-evil deal going down around Sunnydale, and not only was she cool with it, but she actually helped in a real way.

"Sorry," Miss Calendar apologized. "Giles wanted me to tell you that there's been a change of plans. He wants to meet you someplace near his house." She shrugged. "I guess he had to run home and get a book or something."

Buffy blinked. " 'Cause heaven knows there aren't enough books in the library."

Loyally, Miss Calendar replied, "He's very thorough."

"Which is not to bag," Buffy said quickly, not wanting to sound catty. After all, he was doing all this research to protect Angel. "It's kind of manly in an obsessive-compulsive kind of way, don't' you think?"

"Mmm-hmm. You know, my car's here," the teacher answered, effectively brushing the question away. "Why don't I drive you?"

"Okay," Buffy said.

They got in Miss Calendar's classic VW Beetle. Buffy thought the old car was really cool. *Once I get my driver's license, maybe I could get a car,* she thought. *Right. With all that money I make at my after-school Slaying gig.*

The teacher started driving through narrow dark alleys and not really anywhere near Giles's place. Buffy scanned their surroundings, fairly confused.

"We're going to the Bronze?" she queried.

"I'm not sure." Miss Calendar kept her eyes on the road. "Giles gave me an address. I'm just following his directions."

There was a loading dock just up ahead. A large white truck was parked there, and three suspicious-looking guys were loading a rectangular box.

"This looks funky. Stop for a sec," Buffy requested.

Miss Calendar slowed, but didn't immediately stop. "No, Buffy," she said tentatively. "Maybe you shouldn't."

Buffy unlatched the door. "Sorry." She shrugged. "Sacred duty, yada yada yada."

She opened the car door and stepped out as Miss Calendar, left behind, murmured, "What is this?"

Buffy walked toward the truck. As she passed the driver's side door, one of the possibly bad guys on the loading dock moved beneath an overhanging light. Buffy recognized him as the vampire Dalton, a timid little minion of Spike's.

Buffy shook her head and sighed. "Every time I see you, you're stealing something."

Upon seeing her, Dalton growled.

Buffy continued, "You really should speak to somebody about this klepto issue."

The truck engine roared to life. Buffy turned her head to see what was going on. Dalton took advantage to finish carrying his burden into the truckbed, just as the driver's door opened and a vampire in a plaid shirt kicked at Buffy's chest.

She reached into the cab of the truck, grabbed the plaid shirt, and yanked him out. He fell to the ground; when he stood, she punched him so hard he did a backflip.

She stood with her back toward the truck, close to the cab, and readied herself for his next move. Then another attacker reached down from the truckbed and hoisted her up by her shoulders, pinning back her arms as he flung her into the truck. This guy was dressed in forever plaid, too. She used his own momentum against him, pushing him backward against a pile of boxes against the wooden slats, then breaking his grip and headbutting him.

By then, the driver was on board—so to speak—and he came at her, swinging. They exchanged blows; she got in a few good ones and he finally fell, just as the one she had headbutted got back into the game and tried to attack her from behind. But she got to him first, and flung him on top of his good buddy, who was still down for the count.

Inside the Bronze, Angel and the others hid, waiting to spring out and surprise Buffy. Impatiently, Angel murmured, "Where is she?" as the others peered over the pool table, which was laden with Cordelia's chips and dips, some purple and lavender napkins and plates, and the pool balls nicely arranged in a star.

"*Ssh,*" Willow said anxiously. "I think I hear her coming."

At just that moment, Buffy punched one of the wooden boards that made up the truck's walls, broke off a section, and staked the oncoming vamp. Good buddy number two grabbed her up, carried her to the wall of the building, and flung her against it. It hurt a lot as she slammed into it and tumbled to the ground.

Angel had just begun to realize that the strange sounds they were hearing was a fight when Buffy and a vampire in a plaid shirt crashed through the window and landed on the stage.

Glass flew everywhere. Buffy and the vampire battled savagely as everyone rushed from their hiding places.

Then she grabbed a drumstick from the Bronze's house kit and staked the guy.

Dustorama.

There was a long stunned beat as everyone stared. Then Cordelia popped up from behind the cake and yelled, "Surprise!"

Everyone turned and looked at her.

It was Oz who drawled, "That pretty much sums it up."

Buffy jumped off the stage as Angel and Giles moved toward her. Angel said anxiously, "Buffy, are you okay?"

Equally concerned, Giles spoke up. "Yes, what happened?"

She gestured behind herself. "There were these vamps outside . . ." She looked around. "What's going on?"

A bit lamely, Giles said, "Surprise party." He blew his noisemaker.

"Happy birthday," Cordelia chirped sweetly.

Giles tossed his noisemaker over his shoulder.

Buffy lit up. "You guys did all this for me?" She looked at Giles, who smiled faintly, and then at Angel, adoringly. "That is so sweet!"

As if he couldn't let go of it, Angel said, "You're sure you're okay?"

"Yes. I'm fine," she assured him.

Oz was still staring at the spot where the vampire had exploded. Willow came up to him.

"Are *you* okay?"

"Yeah." He looked around at the group. "Hey, did everybody just see that guy turn into dust?"

Willow hesitated. "Uh, sort of."

Xander stepped forward with a "jig's-up" look. "Yep.

Vampires are real," he intoned, as if repeating a very old story. "Lot of 'em live in Sunnydale; Willow'll fill you in."

Willow said gently, "I know it's hard to accept at first."

Oz cut her off. "Actually, it explains a lot." However, he still looked fairly stunned.

Miss Calendar came in the door, struggling under the weight of the box Dalton had been loading onto the truck. She said, "Hey, can somebody give me a hand here?"

Angel, Buffy, and Giles moved to help her, putting the box down on a tall white table.

"Those creeps left it behind," Miss Calendar added.

Buffy cocked her head. "What is it?"

"I have no idea," Giles told her. "Can it be opened?"

Buffy moved her hands under the lid.

"Yeah. It feels like there's a release right here."

She clicked it. Together, she and Giles pulled up the lid.

Inside lay a powerful arm and hand encased in a thick gauntlet of some sort.

Buffy turned to the others and frowned in astonishment. Then, without warning, the arm shot from the box, grabbed Buffy by the neck, and squeezed the breath right out of her.

CHAPTER 3

The living arm choked Buffy as she fought to pull its fingers from her neck. Angel rushed to help, struggling with the macabre thing, finally managing to pry one finger loose. Then another, and another, until he wrestled it back into the box. As Buffy doubled over, coughing, he and Giles slammed the lid into place.

There was a moment of stunned silence. Sounding more freaked than witty, Xander said, "Clearly, the Hellmouth's answer to 'What do you get the Slayer who has everything?' "

"Good heavens," Giles said. "Buffy, are you all right?"

Angel led Buffy away from the table. She rasped, "Man, that thing had major grip."

"What—what *was* that?" Willow asked anxiously.

Matter of factly, Oz replied, "It looked like an arm."

44

Angel's face was grave as he stared at the box. "It can't be," he said quietly. "She wouldn't."

Xander gave him a sharp look. "What? The vamp's version of 'snakes in a can'? Or do you care to share?"

Buffy could tell Angel was freaked in the extreme. "Angel?" she prodded.

Angel looked over at the box again. "It's a legend. Way before my time. Of a demon brought forth to rid the earth of the plague of humanity."

He walked toward Giles and the box. "To separate the righteous from the wicked, and burn the righteous down. They called him the Judge."

Buffy registered that this registered with Giles.

"The Judge," her Watcher said, a bit breathlessly. "This is he?"

"Well, not all of him," Angel replied.

Buffy waved her hand. "Uh, still needing backstory here?"

Giles looked over his shoulder at her. "He couldn't be killed." He looked at Angel for confirmation. "Yes?"

When Angel nodded, Giles continued. "An army was sent against him. Most of them died, but finally they were able to dismember him. But not kill him."

Angel took up the story. "The pieces were scattered. Buried in every corner of the earth."

Miss Calendar said, "So all these parts are being brought here—"

"By Drusilla," Buffy said. "The vamps outside were Spike's men."

"She's just crazy enough to do it." Angel looked even more worried.

And he should know, Buffy thought. *He's the one who drove her crazy. When he was Angelus, he hung with her. To put it politely.*

"Do what?" Willow's voice rose. "Reassemble the Judge?"

"And bring forth Armageddon," Angel finished.

There was a long silence. Then Cordelia piped up, "Is anyone else going to have cake?"

She had no takers.

Giles moved into strategy mode. "We need to get this out of town."

"Angel," Miss Calendar said immediately.

Buffy blinked. "What?"

Miss Calendar stepped up, slightly behind and between Angel and Buffy. She looked at Angel and said firmly, "You have to do it. You're the only one who can protect this thing."

"What about me?" Buffy asked.

Miss Calendar shrugged. "What, you're just going to skip town for a few months?"

"Months?" Buffy echoed, taken aback.

"She's right. I have to take this to the remotest region possible." Angel spoke in a low voice, as if he was thinking aloud.

"But that's not months," Buffy interrupted anxiously.

He continued, "I can catch a cargo ship to Asia, maybe trek to Nepal."

Buffy caught his attention. "You know, those newfangled flying machines are really much safer than they used to be."

"I can't fly," he said impatiently. "There's no sure way

to guard against the daylight." Then he looked down and back up at her, his tone softening as he drew closer to her. "I don't like this any more than you do, Buffy. But there's no other choice."

She took that in. It hurt to admit he was right. It hurt a lot.

"When?"

He hesitated. "Tonight. As soon as possible."

It hurt even more.

"But . . . it's my birthday."

He looked down again, and she knew it was hurting him, too. She took absolutely no comfort in that.

Miss Calendar came up between them. "I'll drive you to the docks."

Giles looked at Buffy very sadly.

Drusilla was enraged as she glared at the officious little clerk who had ruined everything.

"You lost it. *You* lost my present," she said in a dangerous, hushed voice.

"I know," Dalton mewled, like the weak creature he was. "I'm sorry."

From his wheelchair, Spike drawled, "That's a bad turn, man. She can't have her fun without the box."

My Spike is so right.

"The Slayer," Dalton blurted. "She came out of nowhere. I—I didn't even see her."

Glaring at him, Dru put her finger to his lips and hissed, "*Sssh.*" Then she ripped his glasses off his face and crushed them beneath the toe of her lovely crimson satin shoe.

She closed her eyes and said, "Make a wish."

"What?"

She made a fist, extended her pointer and middle fingers and aimed them toward his eyes as she grabbed the back of his head. "I'm going to blow out the candles." When he gasped, she smiled brilliantly.

Perhaps there's fun to be had after all.

"You might give him a chance to find your lost treasure," Spike cut in. "He is a wanker, but he's the only one we've got with half a brain. If he fails, you can eat his eyes out of the sockets for all I care."

Dalton said quickly, "I'll get it." She clawed at him, toying with him, amused by his terror. "Please. I swear."

She couldn't quite stop herself, but somehow she managed it, rushing at his eyes one more time, then capping it off with two fists in the air.

She retrieved his ruined glasses and put them on his face. "Okay," she said casually. "Hurry back, then." She patted him on his bald head, and went to sit on Spike's lap.

All too soon, Buffy and Angel reached the docks. Diesel oil filled the air as the cargo ship moored just ahead of them prepared to leave, its engine rattling. Waves hit the pylons beneath Buffy and Angel's feet as they walked slowly toward the ship, hand in hand. The box containing the Judge's arm was on Angel's shoulder.

Lost in misery, Buffy rested her head against his arm and tried to get even closer. Angel touched the crown of her hair with his lips, and she thought she would lose her balance, she was so unhappy.

They got to the gangplank. He put down the box and said, "I should go the rest of the way alone."

Though she was crying, she kept it together. "Okay—"

"I'll be back," he promised. "I will."

"When? Six months? A year? We don't know how long it's going to take. Or if we'll even—" Her voice cracked.

"If we'll even what?" he pushed, making her say it.

"Well, if you haven't noticed, someone pretty much always wants us dead."

"Don't say that. We'll be fine."

She refused to pretend. "We don't know that."

"We *can't* know, Buffy. Nobody can. That's just the deal."

They looked at each other, two people whose lives had completely been altered by time and circumstance. Strong people. Passionate people. People who needed each other desperately.

Then he reached into his pocket and pulled out a small velvet box. He opened it. "I have something for you. For your birthday. I was going to give it to you earlier, but . . ."

It was an exquisite silver ring, dwarfed in his hand, shining in the dock lights. Two hands held a crowned heart. She had never seen anything more exquisite in her life.

"It's beautiful," she said sincerely.

His voice was husky. "My people . . . before I was changed, they exchanged this as a sign of devotion. It's a claddagh ring. The hands represent friendship, the crown represents loyalty. And the heart, well, you know . . ." He smiled hauntingly. "Wear it with the heart pointing toward you, it means you belong to someone. Like this."

He showed her his hand. He was wearing a ring identical to hers. And the heart was pointing toward him.

He belonged to somebody.

To me, she thought. She took his hand and kissed his ring with all the longing of her soul. *Oh, Angel, I love you. I love you with all my heart.*

"Put it on," he urged.

She did. And then there was nothing more to be said, or done. It was time.

"I don't want to do this," she confessed brokenly.

"Me, either."

"So . . . don't go." She was begging him, even though she knew he had to.

He kissed her. She kissed him back, long and bittersweet and needing him to stay, needing so badly for him to be with her, tonight and every night.

They held each other, clinging against time and tide, and then Angel whispered, "Buffy, I—"

Two vampires leaped down from a cargo net over their heads. One attacked Buffy, and the other went for Angel.

Buffy's opponent tossed her to the ground; she rolled backward and sprang to her feet as he threw a few punches; she got off three good ones to his midsection. Meanwhile, Angel flung his attacker into a wild flip, but the vamp quickly recovered and started swinging.

Using the dock rail as a support, Buffy pulled her legs to her chest and kicked her vampire.

While they were both occupied, Dalton dropped from

the net and grabbed the box. At the same time, Angel hit his attacker so hard he slammed into a crate, but he came back for more.

"Angel!" Buffy shouted. "The box!"

Angel pummeled the vamp into submission, finally slamming him onto the wooden dock. He chased Dalton and threw him down.

Buffy thought she'd gotten control of her opponent, catching him around the neck with a string of lights attached to the gangplank. But she was distracted, trying to see if Angel got the box, and her vamp got free and flung her against a wooden barrier. Then he used her momentum to swing her around and fling her off the dock and into the chilly water.

In that moment, Angel had to make a decision: the box or the Slayer. He chose, and the vampire he had fought darted up beside him, grabbed the box, and ran.

Angel shouted, "Buffy!" and plunged in after her.

Everybody was supposed to be reading their research books, but nobody really was. The sleeves of her sweater stretched to cover her fists, Willow stared at her page anxiously as Giles and Xander stared at theirs. Everyone was anxious. The word for the day was anxious.

Or maybe, really, really worried.

Giles flipped over his page and stated the obvious. "They should be back by now."

"Maybe Buffy needed a few minutes to pull herself together," Willow hoped. "Poor Buffy. On her birthday and everything."

Xander nodded. "It's sad. Granted. But let's look at the up side for a moment." He stood. "I mean, what kind of a future could she have really had with him? She's got two jobs. Denny's waitress by day, Slayer by night. Angel's always in front of the tube, with a big old blood belly.

"And he's dreaming of the glory days when Buffy still thought the whole creature of the night routine was a big turn-on." He pointed his finger for emphasis.

Willow frowned. "You've thought way too much about this."

He warmed to the subject. "No, no, that's just the beginning. Have I told you the part where I fly into town in my private jet and take Buffy out for prime rib?"

Buffy rushed into the library. Willow said warningly, "Xander."

Xander was oblivious. "And she cries?"

Giles saw Buffy and got to his feet. "What happened?"

Buffy looked all business. "Dru's guys ambushed us. They got the box."

No joy, Willow thought, her sentiments echoed by Giles's deep sigh.

"Where's Jenny?" Giles asked.

Buffy gestured. "She took Angel to get clothing. I had some here."

Xander looked perturbed. "And we needed clothes because . . ."

"We got wet," Buffy said simply. "Giles, what do we do?"

Giles took off his glasses and paced. "The more I

study the Judge, the less I like him. His touch can literally burn the humanity out of you. A true creature of evil can survive the process. No human ever has."

"What's the problem?" Xander piped up. "We send Cordy to fight this guy and we go for pizza."

Willow wished she could laugh. Buffy totally ignored Xander and walked over to Giles. "Can this guy be stopped? Without an army?"

Giles put his glasses back on, leaned forward, and showed her a couple of lines in one of the books. "'No weapon forged can kill him.' Not very encouraging. If we could only prevent them from assembling him . . ."

"We need to find his weak spots," Buffy said. "And we need to figure out where they'd be keeping him."

Giles sighed. "This could take time."

"We better do a round robin," Willow suggested. "Xander, you go first."

"Good call," Buffy said, as Xander went to the phone.

"Round robin?" Giles echoed, puzzled.

"It's when everybody calls everybody else's mom and tells them they're staying at everybody's house," Willow explained.

"Thus freeing us up for world save-age," Buffy added.

Willow smiled and raised her brows. "And all-night keggers." When Buffy and Giles stared blankly at her, she protested, "What, only Xander gets to make dumb jokes?"

"Mom, hi. Xander," the guy in question said into the phone. "Yeah. Willow and I are going to be studying all night long. So I'm not coming home."

* * *

It was 2 A.M., and they were no closer to a solution than they had been at midnight. Or at 1 A.M.

Xander was exasperated. "I think I read this already."

Playing with her hair as she looked up from the laptop, Willow said, "I can't get over how cool Oz was about all this."

Xander said snippily, "Gee, *I'm* over it."

"You're just jealous because you didn't have a date for the party," she taunted.

"No, I sure didn't."

Willow didn't know that she'd landed a good one. And he was glad she had a honey. On the other hand, he felt kind of conflicted about Willow's change in status. Before, she was old reliable, his chum in all things, and they were both sweetie-free. Not by choice, but by virtue of the fact that they had been branded with the scarlet letter of Nerdatry and blithely ignored by any and all serious potential sweetie material.

His situation with Cordelia, well, that was a very strange thing, wasn't it? 'Cause she'd probably strike him dead if he thought of it as any kind of a "relationship."

Cordy and I hate each other, but we can't keep our hands off each other. We've got this total repulsion-attraction deal that I sure can't explain. Willow would probably pass out if she knew I spend half the day making out with Cordelia Chase in closets and empty classrooms, and the other half thinking about making out with Cordelia Chase in closets and empty classrooms.

As well as in her car.

He stared at the book some more, just to have something to do.

Giles moved from the checkout desk as Angel came down the stairs from the landing.

"Angel? Any luck?" Before Angel could reply, Giles spotted Buffy, her head on his desk in his office, fast asleep. He whispered, "It seems Buffy needed some rest."

The two looked on, Giles with fondness, Angel with love. They moved away.

"Yes," Angel said. "She hasn't been sleeping well. Tossing and turning."

The others stared at him.

He huffed, "She *told* me. Because of her dreams."

That seemed to satisfy them.

Everyone got back to work.

Because of her dreams . . .

In a white gown, Buffy wandered through a candlelit room. The tapers were almost completely burned, wax dripping off ornate candelabra. She passed chairs decorated with dark leaves.

She knew this place. It was an abandoned factory, the lair of Spike and Drusilla. *When they were alive.*

She moved on. In the distance, a shadowy female figure passed by, perhaps leading her, perhaps eluding her. Buffy followed her as best she could . . .

And found herself crouching over a box like the one the arm had come in.

Then she saw that there were several boxes in a circle.

"Now, now," said a voice.

Drusilla. So she is *alive.*

Buffy whirled around.

"Hands off my presents," the mad vampire chastised.

At the top of the stairs, on the catwalk, Drusilla looked triumphantly down on Buffy. Her thin body was draped in a white gown much like Buffy's, and in her hand she held a sharp, sacrificial knife . . . leveled across Angel's throat. As she clasped his back against her chest, the knife gleaming wicked sharp against his flesh, Angel stared at Buffy with the look of someone who knew he was going to die.

"No!" Buffy shouted. "Angel!"

Then she was awake, in the library, and Angel flew into her arms.

"Buffy, it's okay. I'm here. I'm right here," he comforted her. She shut her eyes tightly, but in her mind's eye, she could only stare with helplessness and horror.

She stared with wide eyes in joy and anticipation.

"More music!" Drusilla commanded, clapping her hands.

Descending the staircase in a truly stupendous scarlet satin gown, she swayed to the drone of a demon ballad. She smiled at a guest and touched his shoulder, noted that Dalton was being good about serving the punch, and picked up her long scarves. She made them ripple as she undulated to the rhythm, supremely happy.

"Look what I have for you, ducks," Spike crowed, as he rolled up with another box on his lap.

Dru posed, spreading her scarves like bat wings, then went to him and lifted the treasure from his knees.

"Ah! The best is saved for last." She handed the box to two minions.

With great care, they walked it over to where the boxes had been assembled into a vaguely human shape—two big, square legs, a torso, two arms. The last box was clearly the head.

As soon as they put it into place, the joints of the boxes flared with brilliant light. The sound of energy crackled over the music and Dru cooed in anticipation.

As the light strobed, the front panels of all the boxes opened, revealing a massive, blue-skinned demon. His flesh was leathery and cracked, his face broad and chunky. He was enormous, and crudely put together, as if there had been no need for niceties or details. Energy sizzled all over him, from his armored feet to the four horns on his head. He was absolutely enormous.

His eyes opened. They were completely black, completely soulless. He was a like a machine. A killing machine, that would mow down anyone and everyone in his path.

"He's perfect, my darling," Dru murmured, as she and Spike looked on in awe. She went to her lover and took his hand, adding darkly, "Just what I wanted."

Chapter 4

Right, then. Here comes the Judge.

The blue demon was a truly impressive sight, crude in a machine-like way, and extremely solid—just a bloody, huge, towering Frankenstein monster of a demon. Fabulous horns on his head, four of 'em, growing out in a sort of organic melange of elegant postmodernism and funky eurotrash. The creature oozed death and evil; he was just totally charismatic that way. If you were a good guy, you'd probably wet your knickers just looking at him.

Spike was ever so delighted that they were both on the same side.

The Judge lumbered out of his coffinlike box.

Baby's first steps, Spike thought, admiring the demon's deadly indifference to the fact that it had been reassembled after centuries of lying about in the muck. It was a killing thing, and it existed solely to fulfill its function. So here it was, reporting for duty.

Which is . . . neat.

The Judge looked at him and Dru, and raised his hand as he lurched toward his poodle like he was going to burn her. "You . . ."

Uh-oh. Better nip this in the bud.

Spike rolled forward. "Ho. *Ho*. What's that, mate?"

"You two stink of humanity." The Judge was not so pleased about that. "You share affection and jealousy."

Spike raised his chin. "Yeah. What of it?" he asked defiantly. "Do I have to remind you that we're the ones who brought you here?"

That seemed to give the old boy pause. Then Dru sashayed toward it in that right fetching way of hers and batted her lovely eyes at it.

"Would you like a party favor?" she asked temptingly.

The Judge looked around. Focused on the wanker, Dalton. It pointed at him and said, "This one is full of feeling. He *reads*. Bring him to me."

A couple vampires brought Dalton forward. The wanker started to struggle.

Spike was suspicious. "What's with the bringing, mate? I thought you could just . . . zap people."

The Judge looked eagerly at Dalton. "My full strength will return in time. Until then, I need contact."

It moved in on the terrified little clerk, who was pleading, "No, no!" to Dru's delight. The Judge reached out its hand.

Contact.

Dalton started to shake. And quake. And smoke. And sizzle. Then he burst into a sort of negative blur of himself, flames shooting from inside him, until the fires ate him up and he vanished.

Dru jumped up and down like the charming little girl Spike knew her to be.

"Do it again! Do it again!" she shouted, clutching Spike's hand with glee.

The Judge exhaled, rather like a burp. He looked rather happy, too.

Full of purpose, Buffy crossed the library and picked up her Slayer's bag.

From the landing, Giles called, "Buffy? What's happening?"

Angel followed her. "She had another dream."

She said, "I think I know where Drusilla and Spike are."

"That's very good." Giles came down the stairs while Angel put on his duster. "However, you do need a plan. I know you're concerned, Buffy, but you can't just go off half-cocked."

"I *have* a plan. Angel and I go to the factory and do recon. Figure out how far they've gotten assembling the Judge. You guys check any places the boxes could be coming into town. Shipping yards, airports, anything. We need to stop them from getting all the boxes in one place."

Giles looked abashed, as if he had underestimated her. "Yes, well . . . actually, that's quite a good plan."

She was very focused on her purpose. "This thing is

nasty and it's real, Giles. We can't wait for it to come get us."

She grabbed her bag, and she and Angel left.

Angel and Buffy moved together through the night. They moved well, coordinating their movements without speaking. It was as if they had trained together, or knew each other so well they could anticipate the other's next action. It was exhilarating, like being in combat, and Buffy found herself glancing at him now and then as if to assure herself that they really were as in synch as she thought.

They reached the factory from the skylight overhead, and Buffy and Angel crept along the second-level catwalk. The candles around them were nearly melted down, which was good. They were able to keep pretty well to the shadows.

Below, the monster mash was in full swing. It was like some kind of strange old horror film: vamps in their true, demonic faces, drinking punch, chatting, milling just like the kind of ordinary people who went to the exhibitions Buffy's mother arranged for the art gallery.

"I saw this," Buffy told Angel, as images from the terrible nightmare she'd had in the library took form in the stark reality before her. "The party . . ."

She stopped speaking.

Below them, a towering, ugly blue demon walked into their range of vision, flanked by Spike, in a wheelchair, and Drusilla, who walked behind the creature.

Buffy's blood ran cold as she gazed down at the trio.

Riveted, she watched in horrible fascination as they moved through the room. *That has to be the Judge. And Drusilla and Spike are both alive.*

So not the news I was hoping for.

The demon began looking around, as if searching for something.

"What?" Spike asked it. "What is it?"

It looked straight up at Buffy and Angel and growled.

Angel pulled at Buffy. "We've got to get out of here."

But as they began to run, they were surrounded on either side by vampires. It was no use even trying to fight. They were outnumbered.

Spike's men dragged them down the stairs, to stand before the Judge, and Spike and Dru.

"Well, well," Spike said jovially. "Look what we have here. Crashers."

Buffy gave him a sarcastic smile, but inside she was very scared. She wasn't giving up hope, but things were not looking good for birthday number eighteen. "I'm sure our invitations just got lost in the mail."

"It's delicious," Dru said, licking her long, pale fingers. "I only dreamed you'd come." She growled prettily at Buffy.

Angel struggled and shouted, "Leave her alone!"

"Yeah, that'll work," Spike drawled, taking a drink from a large brown bottle. "Now say pretty please."

The Judge appraised Buffy. "The girl."

Buffy held her breath and worked to keep her cool. *I'm the Slayer,* she reminded herself. *What's impossible for other other people is not impossible for me.*

"Chilling, isn't it?" Dru chirruped, her eyes filled with

hatred even though she was smiling. "She's so full of good intention."

"Take me," Angel demanded, jumping in front of Buffy.

"No!" Buffy shouted.

"Take me instead of her," Angel demanded, as his captors yanked at him.

In his wheelchair, Spike raised his arm. "You're not clear on the concept, pal." His voice was deadly and cruel. "There is no 'instead.' Just 'first' and 'second.' "

"And if you go first," Dru pointed out, "you won't get to watch the Slayer die."

Angel renewed his struggle, fighting to work himself free. But he was held fast. Furious, he watched as the Judge slowly extended his hand and walked toward Buffy. As frightened as she was, she was keeping her cool, and for that Angel was grateful. *If I could just find a way to stop it . . .*

Then he spied a cluster of TVs chained overhead, like some kind of avant-garde video hookup in a dance club. The whole thing was held in place by a couple of cogs attached to chains. *If I can just get loose for a second . . .*

The Judge reached Buffy and held out his hand. Angel knew what he could do to her. He had never seen any of the Judge's handiwork, but it was still whispered of in the darkness, by creatures who feared nothing else on earth or in hell.

Buffy, Slayer-born and Watcher-trained, reared back and kicked the demon's armored chest. The Chosen One would no more willingly submit to a death sentence than she would allow anyone else to die in her place.

"Don't touch him!" Angel bellowed, but she already had. For one terrifying second he assumed she would burn into nothing. But she was still alive, and apparently uninjured.

In the confusion that followed as the vampires also waited for her annihilation, Angel broke free. Before any of them had a chance to react, he raced to the wall where the chain that suspended the TVs from the ceiling was attached. He unfastened it; as the counterweight was thrown off, the TVs came sailing down like a cascade of granite boulders.

Sparking and sizzling, they crashed down in front of the Judge with such force that they broke through the trapdoor in the concrete floor.

Chaos reigned, and Buffy seized the advantage. She flung her guards away from herself. She ran into Angel's arms, indicated the escape route, and cried, "This way!"

Without a moment's hesitation, they both leaped into the hole while Drusilla, livid, yelled to her minions, "Go!"

Buffy and Angel landed in a sewer. They slogged through the muck until they found an opened utility door. Moving fast, not needing to speak, they darted inside and shut the door behind them. Two of Spike and Dru's lackeys splashed into the wastewater soon after. The two were hot on their trail, but as they raced past, they didn't see the closed door, and moved on.

As soon as it was safe, Buffy and Angel reemerged into the tunnel. There was a ladder nearby, leading to the street overhead.

A driving ran soaked Buffy to the skin as she pushed the manhole cover out of the way. By the time Angel got out behind her, she was shivering.

"Come on," he said over the thunder. "We need to get inside."

They ran to his apartment. She waited while he let her in. The muted light made her feel colder as she stood trembling in the center of the room.

He pulled off his duster and turned to her, stroking her shoulders. "You're shaking like a leaf," he said.

She nodded. "C—cold."

"Let me get you something." He went to his dresser and got out a bulky white sweater and a pair of sweats. Handing them to her, he told her. "Put these on and get under the covers. Just to warm up."

A little hesitantly, she walked toward his neatly made bed. Stood in front of it for just a second before she sat down on the mattress with the bundle of fresh clothes. The coverlet and pillow cases were scarlet. The rain made a drizzling pattern on the wall. Distant thunder rumbled.

Angel faced her. When she looked up and him, he must have realized he was staring at her. He said, "Sorry," and turned away.

Still, he was near. And she was self-conscious as she unbuttoned the drenched cardigan of her twin set. As she drew out her left arm, she winced as something burned across her shoulder.

"What?"

"Oh, um. I—I just have a cut or something," she said, as she finished taking off her sweater.

"Can I . . . let me see."

"Okay." She arranged the sweater across her front so that she was covered.

Then Angel sat behind her on the bed as she turned to show him her back.

His fingers touched her shoulder as he pulled the strap of her camisole aside. His touch was gentle. Both hands moved over her upper back.

"It's already closed," he said hoarsely. "You're fine."

Neither moved. Buffy felt herself trembling harder. She heard Angel swallow hard. She was certain she could hear his heartbeat, or was that her own pulse racing, as his arms cradled her?

She turned, leaned into him. Breathed him in. Tears welled. She was overcome by his nearness, by the fact that she had almost lost him. That tonight, she had thought she might never see him again.

"You almost went away today."

His fingertips stroked her arm as he held her, tension in his body. She knew he was being careful of her; he was struggling against what was taking them both over: the fear and the need.

He said, "We both did."

She started to cry. "Angel, I feel like . . . if I lost you . . ." She caught her breath. "You're right, though. We can't be sure of anything." She moved her lips to the side of his face and wept.

"*Sssh.* I . . ."

She opened her eyes, waited. Moved to face him. "You what?"

"I love you."

And when he said it, her eyes brightened in wonder, though the tears were still there. Angel loved her. It was what she had longed to hear, for such a very long time; and yet, there was tremendous sorrow in his words, and in knowing what she had barely dared to dream. Angel loved her, and now, knowing that, she had so much more to lose.

"I try not to, but I can't stop," he said brokenly.

"Me, too." Her voice cracked as she was overcome with emotion. "I can't, either." She pressed her nose against his.

They kissed. The kiss grew. They were crossing a bridge; they were going somewhere together they had never been before. Buffy's heart pounded with the knowledge that this kiss was the beginning of something much bigger; this was a seal and a promise, and a first step.

Their passion grew. Buffy was starving for the taste of him; she shook with the need of him.

Panting, he pulled away. "Buffy, maybe we shouldn't."

"Don't." She touched his face, held it. "Just kiss me."

Their lips met again, and again.

Angel drew Buffy down into his bed. *She's so beautiful,* he thought. *She feels so amazing. Her skin, her hair . . .* He breathed her in. The scent of her, the satiny softness of her neck, her shoulders. Her hands, caressing him.

Oh, Buffy, Buffy, let me lose myself in you.

Love me.

As they melted into each other, Angel soared with joy. For the first time in 242 years, he had hope of heaven.

The thunder rumbled, and crashed.

Angel bolted awake, unbelievable pain ripping through him. White-hot agony seared him, body and soul.

He panted, fighting it. It was an ancient pain, and he knew what it meant. He knew what was coming, and he was desperate to stop it. He clutched the sheets, heaving, as Buffy slumbered beside him.

No, no, not now . . . it can't be . . . Buffy . . .

Everything was shattering. As he convulsed, he clung to one thought: he had to put as much distance between her and himself as possible.

Protect her . . . oh, my darling, oh, Buffy . . .

Angel dressed and stumbled out into the storm, into the wildness of the night. He clung to the hope that it would stop, that it would not happen. But as he fell to his knees, he knew: his soul was being torn from him once more.

"Buffy!" he shouted.

She was the last thought of the man who loved her.

THE SECOND CHRONICLE:

INNOCENCE

PROLOGUE

Spike rolled his wheelchair along the factory floor. The shadowy, cavernous building had been empty of party guests for quite a long time. Funny how a gate-crashing Slayer and a double-crossing, back-stabbing Judas of a former mate and grandsire could take the fun right out of an evening—if they got away. Now there was that cloud that comes after the music dies, that melancholy that comes over one when they're cleaning up the ashtrays, throwing out the empties, and burying 'em in unmarked graves.

Now it was just him and Dru, and their big blue baby made three.

Irritated, Spike frowned in the direction of the Judge. The bloke had been kneeling with his back to the room for quite a long time, and that didn't make Spike any happier. You ate Spike's crisps and drank his liquor, you

71

did a lot more than pretend you were a bloody door stop, as far as Spike was concerned.

"I'm not happy, pet," he groused to Drusilla, getting angrier because she was flouncing about instead of taking this crisis seriously. "Angel and the Slayer are still alive, they know where we are, they know about the Judge. We should be vacating."

Still dressed in her scarlet party best, his peaches took his hand. "Nonsense. They'll not disturb us here." Then she had to go and ruin the moment by adding, "My Angel is too smart to face the Judge again."

Always with the "my Angel," she was. Okay, right, he made her. He was her big daddy, her sire. But Angelus had left that all behind, while he, Spike, put up with the tantrums and the mood swings and the rest of Dru's high-maintenance schedule . . . and did it with great patience and understanding, if he did say so. Where she got off cooing and rolling her huge, lovely eyes at the very utterance of the syllables of his name—the first two syllables, like Angelus had become some very cool rock star—was bloody bewildering. He would never, ever parade a rival for his affections around Drusilla. Not that there were any. *But still, the point has been made.*

"What's Big Blue up to, anyway? He just sits there," Spike grumbled.

The Judge spoke. "I am preparing."

"Yeah," Spike huffed and let go of Dru's hand. She stayed where she was as he wheeled himself toward the demon. He couldn't give her what for—her bloody insanity got her off scot-free every time—so he decided to take it out on their houseguest. "It's interesting to me that preparing looks a great bit like sitting on your ass. When do we destroy the world already?"

"My strength grows," the Judge informed him. "And with every life I take, it will increase further."

Spike supposed it was time to state the obvious. No one else in the bleeding house seemed to show the slightest bit of initiative in the whole affair. "So let's take some! I'm bored."

Behind him, Drusilla suddenly let out an agonized moan and crumpled to the floor. He jerked his head toward her in alarm.

"Dru?"

She stretched out on the floor, making a terrible weeping, keening like she'd just lost every single thing she'd ever cared about. Spike wheeled toward her.

"Angel," she wept.

Oh, blimey, he thought, but knew he had to keep a lid on it until he found out what was happening. Dru's visions were an integral part of their survival strategy, and as valid as his jealousy of Angelus might be, it was more important to find out what Drusilla meant by sobbing out his name like a dying maiden in an Italian opera.

Spike leaned forward intently. "Darling, do you see something?"

Her eyes lost their focus; she looked dreamy and glowing. Then she broke into smile and began to softly laugh.

The rain poured down. Buffy snuggled cozily against her pillow and reached for Angel.

He wasn't there.

She opened her eyes, remembering where she was, and slowly sat up pulling the sheets across her chest.

Lightning flashed outside as she glanced across the room.

"Angel?" she called, almost a whisper.

But he wasn't there.

The rain poured down, needle-sharp and icy. Lightning crackled; thunder rolled across the black night, mirroring the battle taking place inside Angel.

Outside his apartment, sprawled helplessly in the frigid storm, Angel struggled with the pain, fought to keep himself from flying apart inside.

"Buffy," he rasped, panting, and then it began to happen; he could feel it; and he knew he could not stop it. "Oh, no."

He was losing it all . . . it was like watching someone behead you or brainwash you, only it was much worse. He was becoming everything he loathed. There was nothing he could do about it. No way to stop all the tragedy that would surely follow.

Better I die now, he thought wildly. *Let me die now.*

Buffy, my darling, my love, my life.

If he held on to her name, maybe he could save himself. Maybe he could tread water until the moment passed.

But it was too late. Sinking below the surface of his awareness, he felt his soul tear away and head for the surface, leaving him to be washed in evil, rebaptized into the community of the damned.

He lowered his head in defeat.

Across the alley, a world-weary blond in a leather jacket took a drag on a cigarette. She was the kind of woman who drank whiskey straight around her girlfriends and had an ex-husband back in Westbridge.

She stepped from the doorway where she stood smoking and came toward him, filled with concern and some common-sense bit of caution.

"Are you okay?" she asked. "You want me to call 911?"

There was a silence. Then he got to his feet, his back to her. "No," he replied in a strong, firm voice. "The pain is gone."

She was still concerned, and now less cautious. "You're sure?"

Without warning, he whirled around, displaying his vamp face. Savagely, he buried his teeth into her neck before she had time to react.

Ah, warm, human blood laced with fear. My favorite.

Exhilarated, he lifted his face to the cold, dark night and exhaled her cigarette smoke.

And finished off with a dollop of tasty unfiltered tar and nicotine.

"I feel just fine," he confided to her corpse.

CHAPTER 1

Buffy had snuck into her house a hundred times, on days more brilliant and sunny than this one. She had had such close calls back in Los Angeles they had been the stuff of legend.

But today was the day her mother had to be waiting for her.

She was about a third of the way up the stairs before Joyce called out, "Good morning."

Busted.

As her stomach did a flip, she darted back down the stairs like she had absolutely nothing to hide—which, if she thought about it, was a most unnatural attitude to take with her mother, since she had made it a habit to hide just about everything since holding the big ticket in the Slayer lottery. A little breathless, she said, "Good morning."

"So, did you have fun last night?" Her mother rounded the corner from the dining room into the front hall.

Buffy's eyes widened and she took a step back. Or rather, up, the stair. *Don't retreat. Don't act weirder than usual.*

"Fun?" she echoed shakily, keeping those windows to the soul as big and round and free of guilt as she could manage.

Her mom stayed pleasant, which was a good sign she wasn't noticing Buffy's discomfort.

"At Willow's," Joyce said.

"Yes, yes, fun at Willow's." Nervously, she looped her hair around her ears. She was no longer wet, but she was definitely rumpled. She kept her eyes wide, her smile innocent. "You know, she's a fun machine."

"You hungry?" The perennial mom question, when all Buffy wanted to do was escape her scrutiny.

"Not really." She gestured toward the second floor of their house, where she most desperately wanted to be. "I'm just going to take a shower."

"Well, if you hurry, I'll run you to school." Her mom smiled again.

"Thanks," Buffy said quickly.

Now Joyce took a closer look. She narrowed her eyes and crossed her arms over her chest, cocking her head as she studied Buffy.

"Is something wrong?"

Go for wide eyes. Go for innocence, Buffy told herself. *She doesn't know. She can't tell.*

Can she?

"No," Buffy assured her. "What would be wrong?"

"I don't know. You just look . . ."

Innocent. I look innocent.

Her mother shrugged, gave her head a little shake, and walked back into the kitchen.

Buffy turned and walked back up the stairs, the rip in her sweater the only visible evidence of what had happened last night.

Giles was standing behind the checkout desk when Xander swung into the library. Cordelia was seated fetchingly on top of the counter, a big book on her lap.

"Well, the bus station was a total washout, and may I say what a lovely place to spend the night," Xander groused. "What a vibrant cross-section of Americana."

"No vampires transporting boxes?" Giles asked.

"No, but a four-hundred-pound wino offered to wash my hair," Xander informed him. He turned around and saw Miss Calendar and Willow standing by the book cage. *Two very gloomy women. And Cordy makes three.*

Alarm bells went off. "What's up? Where's Buffy?"

Willow said glumly, "She never checked in."

Giles looked up from a notebook. "If the bus depot is as empty as the docks and the airport—" He sounded very weary, and very worried.

"Come on. Do you think this Judge guy's already been assembled?" Xander asked.

"Yes." Defeated, Giles capped his pen.

"Then Buffy could be . . ." *Can't go there,* Xander thought. *Won't go there.* "We've got to find them." *Don't panic. How can I not panic? This is Buffy. Okay, where did she and Angel say they were going? She had the dream about the party. Giles got all dissy that she didn't have a plan, which she did, and then they split.*

To the factory!

"We've got to go to that place, that factory. That's where they're holed up, right?" He turned to Willow and Miss Calendar. "Let's go."

Cordelia gazed at him in bewilderment. "And do what? Besides be afraid and die?"

"Nobody's asking you to go, Cordelia," Xander retorted. "If the vampires need grooming tips, we'll give you a call."

She lowered her eyes as if she were ashamed.

Yeah. As if.

Giles spoke up. "Cordelia has a point. If Buffy and Angel were . . . harmed, we don't stand to fare much better."

Xander was too pumped to even consider what Giles was saying. Rescue was the only thing on his mind. "Yeah, well those of us who were born with feelings are going to do something about this."

Miss Calendar reproved him. "Xander."

"No. Xander's right," Willow blurted. "My God! You people are all . . . well, I'm upset and I can't think of a mean word right now, but that's what you are and we're going to the factory!" She led the way.

"Yeah," Xander added, trailing behind her.

At that moment, Buffy walked through the library's double doors.

"Buffy!" Willow cried.

Thank God. Xander told her, "We were just going to rescue you."

"Well some of us were." Willow looked pointedly at Giles.

"I would have." He sounded defensive.

Miss Calendar walked up beside Willow. "Where's Angel?"

Buffy looked stricken. She turned to Giles. "He didn't check in with you guys?"

"No," Giles told her.

Cordelia slid off the counter. "What happened?"

Giles took a breath. "The Judge . . . is he?"

"No assembly required," Buffy confirmed wearily. "He's active."

"Damnit." Giles pulled off his glasses.

Buffy continued, "He nearly killed us. Angel got us out."

"Why didn't you call?" Giles asked more gently. *Like a worried dad.* "We thought—"

"Well, uh, we had to hide," Buffy said to the group. "We got stuck in the sewer tunnels, and with the hiding, we split up—and no one's heard from him?" Her voice was little-girl-lost, and as much as Xander was jealous of Dead Boy, he felt for her.

Willow came forward and said soothingly, "I'm sure he'll come by."

"Yeah. I'm sure you're right." Buffy sounded not at all convinced.

"Buffy, the Judge." Giles hesitated, like he didn't want to sound callous. "We must stop him."

"I know." She went right into Slayer mode. *Man, she's cool.*

"What can you tell us?" Giles asked, all ears.

"Not much," she admitted. "I just kicked him, and it was like a sudden fever." *I didn't tell Angel that. He assumed I wasn't affected. That was why I was so woozy when we got to his place.* "If he got his hands on me . . ."

"In time he won't need to," Giles said anxiously. "The stronger he gets, he'll be able to reduce us to charcoal with a look."

"Also?" Buffy added. "Not the prettiest man in town."

Giles sighed in frustration "I'm going to continue researching, look for a weak spot. The rest of you should get to your classes."

"I better go, too," Miss Calendar said, moving toward the door. "I'll go on the Net and search for anything on the Judge."

"Thank you," Giles said sincerely.

Xander paused at the door. "After classes, I'll come back and help you research."

Cordelia began to sweep by him, then stopped for one last arrow. "Yeah, you might find something useful . . . if it's in an I-Can-Read book." She patted his chest.

Xander was taken aback. *Always with the insults.* Then he shrugged it off and went on his way. The Judge could definitely do a lot more harm than Cordy.

Willow walked with Buffy down the corridor as students bustled around them. She asked, "You don't think Angel would have gone after the Judge himself, do you?"

"No. He'd know better than that. Maybe he just needed . . . I don't know." *I can't tell her I slept with him,* Buffy thought. *I can't tell anyone. What would they think? What is he thinking? Where is he?* "I just wish he'd contact me. I need to talk to him."

They went up the stairs, unaware that Miss Calendar lingered behind them, listening and unconsciously tapping her fingers against her mug of herbal tea, deep in thought.

In the factory, Dru was reclining on a long shelf, dreaming, smiling, moaning with pleasure.

"Are we feeling better, then?" Spike asked her.

She sighed and put her hand to her forehead. "I'm naming all the stars."

"You can't see the stars, love," he said, trying to sound patient. She knew her Spike. *He's so . . . earthbound sometimes. It comes from being an earth sign* "That's the ceiling," he went on. "Also, it's day."

She smiled a secret smile. "I can see them. But I've named them all the same name, and there's terrible confusion." She rolled seductively toward him. "I fear there may be a duel."

He leaned his head toward hers. She saw his lovely scars and wanted to reach out and touch them, name them, too.

"Recovered then, have we? Did you see any further? Do you know what happens to Angel?"

"Well, he moves to New York and tries to fulfill that Broadway dream," Angel boomed as he sauntered into the room. Dru raised her head, mesmerized, delighted. "It's tough sledding, but one day he's working in the chorus when the big star twists his ankle."

Oh, blimey, Dru thought. *He's here, my Angel. My dear sire, who let me make Spike for a playmate. And then, perhaps, he got a bit jealous before he turned into such a little "angel." Oh, but they were like two great stags when we ran together, two bucks, just knocking horns constantly. They were both so macho.*

I so adored it.

Then we lost Angel to goodness and good deeds. Despite all their rivalry, Spike was more disappointed than I. He really looked up to Angelus, tried to copy his barbarity. Never quite managed it.

No one could ever compare to Angelus for barbarity. It was his passion.

Rather, one of them . . .

Spike said in his wonderful cold, deadly voice, "You don't give up, do you?"

Angel became very grave. "As long as there is injustice in this world, as scum like you is walking—or well, rolling," he laughed, "the streets, I'll be around. Look over your shoulder. I'll be there."

"Yeah, uh, Angel. Look over *your* shoulder."

The Judge was the one doing the touching. He splayed his hand over Angel's chest. Dru looked on, fascinated, thrilled, getting on her hands and knees like a lioness.

"Hurts, doesn't it?" Spike taunted.

"Well, you know, it kind of itches a little," Angel tossed off, wincing. But nothing else happened. Dru kept waiting for the immolation, recalling nights of cheering on fireworks displays with just the same amount of anticipation.

Her Spike was angry. "Don't just stand there. Burn him!"

Angel made a face. He was obviously enjoying himself. "Gee, maybe he's broken."

"What the hell is going on?" Spike demanded.

Dru got it. She *knew*.

"This one cannot be burned. He is clean," the Judge said, vaguely disappointed.

"Clean? You mean he's—" Spike said, slowly coming along to the notion.

"There is no humanity in him." The Judge turned away, losing interest.

Angel preened. "Couldn't have said it better myself."

"Angel," Dru breathed, awash in delirious joy.

Angel grinned at her. Looked deep into her eyes with a sinister, wonderful gleam. They were connecting right here, and right now, and she could barely contain herself.

"Yeah, baby," he said, "I'm back."

CHAPTER 2

Angelus—for that was his original name, after all, and who he really was now—so loved the looks of astonishment on the faces of Dru and Spike. *They're almost speechless. They really don't know what to think.*

"It's really true?" Spike asked, all jazzed up like a kid who's just seen Santa . . . lying in the gutter with two holes in his neck.

Angelus preened. "It's really true."

Dru crouched. Her eyes were shining, her teeth glittered. Every movement invited him, welcomed him. *Yeah, I'll be there,* Angelus thought lustfully. *Asap.*

"You've come home," she cooed.

"No more of this 'I've got a soul' crap?" Spike pressed, as if he was still not sure about this new deal. As if the emperor's clothes might just fall off.

Dru would like that, wouldn't you, baby?

"What can I say?" Angelus said, taking out a match and running it down the length of the tabletop. "I was going through a phase." He lit a cigarette and put it in his mouth.

"This is great!" Spike cried. "This is so great."

Dru tottered along the length of the table like a tightrope walker.

"Everything in my head is singing," she rejoiced. Dreamily, she moved her head in a slow circle. Then she darted toward Angelus and extended her hand. He clasped it and helped her off the table, chuckling as she said, "We're family again. We'll feed." At the exact same time, they snapped their jaws at each other.

"And we'll play." She leaned toward Spike and kissed the space between them. *I'm still yours, my darling,* she thought.

Mostly.

Spike chuckled, savoring her attention. "I gotta tell you, it made me sick to my stomach seeing you being the Slayer's lap dog."

Angelus flared with anger, growling, grabbing Spike's lapels. For an instant or two, his thought was to kill his friend. Then he got control and made a show of kissing his old hunting partner on the forehead.

Spike burst into high laughter, a bit grating, truth be told. Dru's amused reaction was more like honey, thick and amber-sweet.

"How did this happen?" Her eyes shone. She was so very, very happy to have him back.

And I will be happy to have you, as well, he thought.

"You wouldn't believe me if I told you." *I only slept with the enemy, that's all.*

"Who cares?" Spike crowed. "What matters is now he's back. Now it's four against one, which are the kind of odds I like to play."

"Pssst." Dru leaned forward and said to Angelus in a happily guilty, hushed voice, "We're going to destroy the world. Want to come?"

Spike laid a possessive hand on her belly. She liked that, put her own hand over it. Angelus took it all in, making up his game board, planning his moves. *You don't get to be the Scourge of Europe unless you stay a few steps ahead of your pawns.*

"Yeah, destroying the world. Great." He casually examined his cigarette, looked back at their proud, shining little faces. "I'm really more interested in the Slayer."

"Well, she's *in* the world, so that should work out," Spike said dryly, with just a soupçon of hostility thrown in to keep things interesting.

Angelus said, "Give me tonight."

"What do you mean?" Spike asked.

"Lay low for a night." He flicked his cigarette. "Let me work on her. I guarantee by the time you go public, she won't be anything resembling a threat." He grinned in anticipation of the torture he would inflict on Buffy Summers.

Spike was delighted. *Maybe until I said that, he didn't believe I was really myself again,* Angelus guessed.

"You've really got a yen to hurt this girl, haven't you?"

"She made me feel like a human being." Angelus lost his lightheartedness as hatred seethed through him.

"I like seeing you. And the part at the end of the night when we say goodbye, it's . . . getting harder."

—*Buffy*

"Happy Birthday, Buffy."
—*Drusilla*

"I love you. I try not to, but I can't stop—"

—*Angel*

"Yeah, baby. I'm back."

—*Angel*

"She made me feel like a human being. That's not the kind of thing you just forgive."

—*Angel*

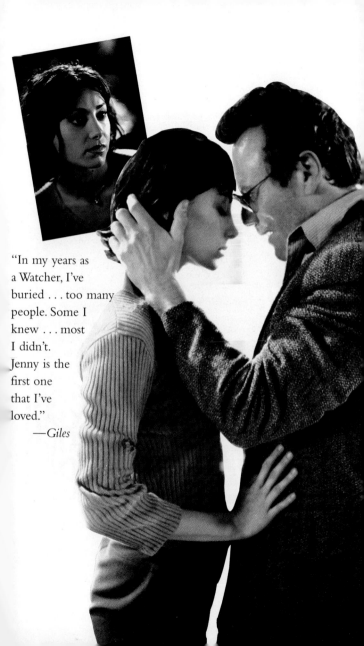

"In my years as a Watcher, I've buried . . . too many people. Some I knew . . . most I didn't. Jenny is the first one that I've loved."

—*Giles*

"I'm sorry I couldn't kill him for you . . . for her . . .
when I had the chance."

—*Buffy*

"That's not the kind of thing you just forgive."

Dru glowed at him. Positively glowed.

In the Sunnydale High School library, Willow was on the phone with Buffy. And Buffy was wigged.

"Okay . . . no, he didn't," Willow said on her end. "But I'm sure he'll . . . Buffy, he probably has some plan and he's trying to protect you. Well, I don't know what, I'm not in on the plan, it's his plan. No. Don't even say that. Angel is not dead."

But we can all hope, Xander thought. *Whoa, not bitter. And it would break Buffy's heart if someone dusted Angel.*

Xander looked up from his assigned research book. "Say hi for me."

Willow frowned at his extreme tackiness. "Yes, we'll be here. Of course. Okay. Bye."

She hung up and looked askance at her best friend since childhood. " 'Say hi for me?' "

Xander let it go by. The I'm-jealous-of-Angel bit was theoretically of the past, especially now that he was making out on a regular basis with a real, live girl. "What's the word?"

Willow was worried. "She's checked every place she could think of. She even beat up Willy the Snitch a couple times. Angel's vanished."

Behind her, Giles said from his office, "But he does do that on occasion, no?"

"Yeah, but she's extra wigged this time," she told him. Then she turned back to Xander. "I guess 'cause of her dreams. God, what if something really happened to him?"

Xander kept his gaze on his book as Giles asked, "Is she going to join us here?"

"Yes. She's just stopping at home first." Frowning, Willow returned to the big, thick book she was slogging through.

"*Nada,*" Xander groused, slamming his book shut. He slid off his stool and went to get another.

Here she is, Miss Cordelia. The ice queen was in the stacks, reading.

Xander said, as neutrally as possible, "Did you find anything?"

"This book mentions the Judge, but nothing useful." She sounded discouraged. "Big scary, no weapon forged can stop him, took an army to take him down, blah, blah, blah."

"We need some insight. A weak spot," he ventured.

"Well, we're not going to find it here." She shut the book and put it back on the shelf. Then she smoothed back her hair, perhaps not realizing just how incredibly sexy that was.

Xander came up behind her and she turned around to face him. "I'm sorry I snapped at you before."

She grimaced. "Well, I'm reeling from *that* new experience."

"I was crazed. I wasn't thinking." *And I'm being honest here, Cordy, which is the kind of thing you claim as your own.*

"I know. You were too busy rushing off to die for your beloved Buffy." She sounded hurt. "You'd never die for *me.*" There was a question mark on the end of that declarative statement.

"I might die *from* you." He gave her an intimate grin. "Does that get me any points?"

She blinked. "No."

Harsh. "Come on," he cajoled, just a tad, because as a rule, Cordelia was not cajoleable. "Can't we just kiss and make up?"

She closed her eyes. "I don't want to make up." She looked very stern, and then grabbed his arm. "But I'm okay with the other part." And wrinkled her nose.

They smiled at each other, dropping the feisty thing, and she cupped the side of his face as they kissed. She giggled a little, very softly, and Xander lost himself in the softness of her lips. *Ach, du lieber. We're haben der smoochies.* Cordelia, when yielding, was gentle and sweet. Her arm draped over his shoulder, her hand now on the back of his neck—this was a very different Cordy.

One who needs another kiss from me. And another.

She smiled at him as they broke apart, both of them grinning.

And then, Xander realized they were not alone.

Willow was watching them, and she looked as though he had socked her in the stomach.

"Willow! We were just—" He chased after her.

Cordy stayed behind, thinking, *Oh, no, it's out.*

Xander dashed after his best buddy, the first girl to see him cry—well, okay, the only girl, when he lost his G.I. Joe—the girl he had nearly drowned when they had bobbed for apples on a long-ago Halloween.

"Willow, come on!"

She screeched to a halt beside the trophy case in the

main hall and whirled on him. "I knew it! I knew it!" She shook her finger at him. "Well, not 'knew it' in the sense of having the slightest idea, but I knew there was something I didn't know. You two were fighting way too much. It's not natural."

Xander helplessly held out his hands. "I know it's weird."

"Weird? It's against all the laws of God and man! It's *Cordelia!*" Willow was so angry she was sputtering. "Remember the 'we hate Cordelia club,' of which you are the treasurer?"

"I was going to tell you—"

"Gee, what stopped you? Could it be *shame?*" she sniped.

He lowered his voice a half-octave. *Things are getting too shrill. Which means our voices may carry. All the way back into the library.*

"All right, let's overreact, shall we?"

She gestured angrily. "But I'm—"

"We were kissing. It doesn't mean that much." *Which is bizarre, but true. At least, I think it is.*

And then she deflated. Her face filled with pain. "No," she said miserably. "It just means you'd rather be with someone you hate, than be with me."

Her voice cracked on the word, "me."

So did Xander's heart.

She turned and ran away.

He thought to run after her and try to make things right.

But why? It's true.

* * *

Buffy trudged to the front door of her house. She stood and stared at the three rectangles of glass. Her heart pounded. She was numb with fear and dizzying confusion.

She would not go in. She would not allow herself to be safe when she had no idea if Angel was alive or dead.

Resolutely, she turned and walked back into the night.

A short time later, she let herself into his apartment. As always, it was muted. The soft lighting gave an antique sheen to the objects in the room—the statue in the case, the chair that reminded her of old movies about New York.

Then she saw the crimson pillows, the coverlet. The things he had given her to wear, which she had neatly folded and left on his bed.

His bed.

Where he . . .

Where we . . .

She turned at a noise and saw him shirtless, emerging from behind a screen, in black leather pants, putting on his chain.

"Angel!" Joyfully, she ran to him and threw her arms around him. It was almost like a dream, she was so glad to see him. It made her feel like she was spinning.

"Hey," he said pleasantly.

"Oh, Angel, oh, God, I was so worried." Held him so tightly she would never be able to let him go. *Alive. He's okay. He's okay!*

"Didn't mean to frighten you." He gave her a little smile.

"Where did you go?" Tears of relief streamed down her face.

"Been around."

She hugged him again. *Alive. Safe. Thank God.* "I was freaking out. You just disappeared," she reproved him, unable to keep the happiness out of her voice, managing just a touch of possessive lecture mode. *Which I get to do now that we're, um, together.*

"What? I took off," he said, with a distinct lack of concern.

"But you didn't say anything," she said, puzzled. "You just left."

He started putting on a gray silk shirt. He smirked at her and said, "Yeah, like I really wanted to stick around after *that.*"

Buffy blinked, as stunned as if he had slapped her. "Wh—*what?*"

"You've got a lot to learn about men, kiddo. Although I guess you proved that last night." He made a little face, as if he was embarrassed for her.

She went completely numb. *This can't be happening. He couldn't have said what I think he just said.*

"What are you saying?"

"Let's not make an issue out of it, okay? In fact, let's not talk about it at all." He shrugged. "Hey, it happened."

"I don't understand." She could barely get the words out. She had come to him in trust. In love. But the way he was acting . . . it was . . .

"Was it me?" she asked in a small voice. "Was I . . . not good?"

He laughed heartily. "You were great. Really." He leered at her. "I thought you were a pro."

She clenched her jaw to keep from bursting into tears. Her stomach was clenching. She was shaking.

"How can you say these things to me?" she asked brokenly.

"Lighten up. It was a good time." He rolled his eyes. "Doesn't mean we have to make a big deal."

"It *is* a big deal!" she cried. "It's—it's—"

"It's what? Bells ringing? Fireworks?" he mocked. "A dulcet choir of pretty little birdies?" He sniggered. "Come on, Buffy." He leaned into her, reaching to chuck her under the chin. "It's not like I've never been there before."

She took a step back. "Don't touch me," she whispered.

He smirked. "I should have known you wouldn't be able to handle it."

"Angel!" She stared at him, her heart reaching out to him one more time. Unable to capitulate to his cruelty. Unable to accept that it was her boyfriend acting like this. "I love you."

"Love ya too," he drawled. He went to the door, opened it, his back to her. "I'll call you." He sauntered out. He didn't even look over his shoulder at her.

Staring after him, she trembled with pain and shock.

In the cold, dark room, the world had just ended.

Jenny sat in the overstuffed armchair in her uncle's furnished room. She was there to look for answers. Thus far, he was the one asking the questions.

"Do you know what it is, this thing called vengeance?"

"Uncle, I have served you," she said urgently, "I've been faithful. I need to know."

He ignored her. "To the modern man, vengeance is an idea, a word. Payback. One thing for another, like commerce." He raised his finger. "Not with us. Vengeance is a living thing. It passes through generations. It commands. It kills."

She tried again. *I have to make him see,* she thought. *We need his help.*

"You told me to watch Angel. You told me to keep him from the Slayer. I tried. But there are other factors, there are terrible things happening here that we cannot control."

"We control nothing," he said incredulously. "We are not wizards, Janna. We merely play our part."

She looked up at him, willing him to be reasonable, to really listen to her.

"Angel could be of help to us. He may be the only chance we've got to stop the Judge."

"It is too late for that." His lined face was sad as he sat on his narrow bed.

She was chilled. "Why?"

"The curse. Angel was meant to suffer. Not to live as human. One moment of true happiness, of contentment . . . one moment where the soul that we restored no longer plagues his thoughts—and that soul is taken from him."

"Then somehow if . . . if it's happened . . ." She lowered her eyes as she processed her thoughts . . . *if he has found happiness with Buffy* . . . "Then Angelus is back."

"I hoped to stop it. But I realize now it was arranged to be so." His voice was hollow with resignation.

"Buffy loves him." It was a plea.

"And now she will have to kill him." It was a fact.

Jenny jumped to her feet. "Unless he kills her first! Uncle, this is insanity!" She gestured with her hands, unable to believe the way he just sat there, just looked at her. Just let this happen. "People are going to *die.*"

"Yes. It is not justice that we serve. It is vengeance." He said it calmly. She could see there was no dissuading him. The path had been chosen generations ago, and he would not stray from it.

She exhaled, angry and defeated. "You're a fool. We're all fools."

She grabbed her purse and left.

He made no move to stop her.

Xander came out of the bathroom as Willow was walking slowly down the corridor, toward the library.

"Will!" he called.

She hugged herself and faced him. "Hey," she said coolly. He inclined his head, accepting the distance she was putting between them.

"Where did you go?"

"Home."

"I'm glad you came back," he said honestly. "We can't do this without you."

She didn't smile. "Let's get this straight." Her tone was determined and he could tell she was still angry and hurt. "I don't understand it. I don't want to understand it.

You have gross emotional problems and things are *not* okay between us."

He accepted that also. He didn't like it, and it hurt.

"But what's happening right now is more important than that," she finished with resignation.

"Okay." *Oh Will,* he wanted to say, *I'm sorry. I didn't mean for it to happen. I never meant for it to happen.*

But she became all business, and the time to speak like that was past. *For now,* he promised himself. *We'll talk about it later.*

"What about the Judge? Where do we stand?" Willow asked.

"On a pile of really boring books that say exactly the same thing," he admitted.

"Let me guess. 'No weapon forged . . .' "

" 'It took an army . . .' "

"Huh. Yeah, where's an army when you need one?" she asked, rather bitterly.

Xander blinked. Hard. *Army?*

"What?" Willow asked.

"Whoa. Whoa." His mind was racing. "I think I'm having a thought. Yeah. Yeah, that's a thought. Now I'm having a plan." *Cool. And possibly—*

The lights in the hallway went out.

Xander said, "And now I'm having a wiggins."

"What's going on?" Willow asked anxiously.

He took her arm and they both started down the corridor as Xander said, "Let's get back to the library."

"Willow? Xander?" a voice called softly behind them.

They turned. The muted silhouette of a tall guy stood beside the illuminated trophy case.

"Angel," Xander said, relieved that it was a friend. *Sort of a friend.*

"Thank God you're okay!" Willow cried. "Did you see Buffy?"

"Yeah." Angel sounded calm and collected. He looked around. "What's up with the lights?"

"I don't know," Xander said, gesturing for Angel's attention. "Listen I have an idea—"

"Forget about that. I've got something to show you." He gestured toward the closed doors behind him with his shoulder.

"Show us?" Willow sounded as puzzled as Xander.

"Yes. Xander, go get the others."

Xander moved into action. "Okay."

He took off.

"And Willow, come here," Angel said.

Willow walked toward him. "What is it, Angel?"

"It's amazing," he promised.

Willow kept walking.

Further down the corridor, beyond the set of doors, a strange feeling passed through Xander. *Something's not right.*

He turned, frowned, and started back toward where he had left Willow with Angel.

Willow had almost reached Angel.

"Willow, get away from him." It was Miss Calendar.

"What?" Willow faced her. The dark-haired teacher was holding a large wooden cross.

"Walk to me," she said firmly.

Willow didn't get it. Hesitating in midstep, she said, "What are you talking about?"

Then Angel growled and grabbed her up, one hand around her neck, the other clenching her shoulder. She struggled, completely freaked, as he practically choked the breath out of her.

Xander ran through the doors and skidded to a stop beside Miss Calendar.

"Don't do that!" he shouted.

"Oh, I think I do that," Angel said viciously.

Willow looked up at him. He was in full vamp face, his eyes glowing golden. "Angel . . ." she pleaded.

"He's not Angel anymore. Are you?" Miss Calendar asked in a cold, hard voice.

"Wrong. I *am* Angel." Even his voice was different— mean, savage. "At last."

"Oh, my God," Xander breathed, getting it.

"I've got a message for Buffy," Angel continued, squeezing harder.

"Then why don't you give it to me yourself?"

Angel pulled Willow with him as he whirled around to face Buffy, who looked hard and fierce and thoroughly ready to kill him if he didn't let go of Willow. Willow allowed herself to hope that she was going to live through this. But Angel was gripping her really, really hard.

"Well, it's not really the kind of message you tell," Angel informed Buffy. "It sort of involves finding the bodies of all your friends." He gave Willow another hard squeeze. She cried out hoarsely, terrified.

* * *

Buffy was trying to be strong, but she was shaking. Angel was inches away from strangling Willow right in front of her.

"This can't be you," she said, staring at the wild creature who was menacing her friend.

"We've already covered that subject," he flung at her.

She couldn't keep the pain from her face and her voice as she fought to get through to him. "Angel, there must be some part of you inside that still remembers who you are." *Please, Angel. Please, stop this.*

"Dream on, *schoolgirl,*" he sneered. "Your boyfriend is dead. You're all gonna join him."

Behind Angel, Xander took the cross from Miss Calendar and began advancing on the vampire.

"Leave Willow alone and deal with me," Buffy ordered Angel.

"But she's so cute." He pinched Willow's cheek. Willow gasped. "And helpless." His tone grew husky, insinuating. His claddagh ring caught the glint of the light, and Buffy was almost sick. "It's really a turn-on."

Xander made his move. He darted around Angel's right and shoved the cross in Angel's face. Angel roared with fury and flung Willow at Xander. They both slammed into the wall and collapsed to the floor.

Furious, Angel advanced on Buffy, grabbing her, looming over her. He brought his face close to hers and whispered, "Things are about to get very interesting."

Then he kissed her hard, a kiss filled with contempt and loathing, then threw her away from himself. Buffy hit the floor as her back smacked the wall. In shock, she stared while Angel backed through the exit doors, obviously savoring his handiwork, and left.

Xander and Willow ran to her. "Buffy," Xander demanded urgently, "are you okay?"

She made no answer. She only kept staring.

Xander tried again. "Buffy?"

She couldn't speak.

CHAPTER 3

After Angel split, everyone convened in the library. Giles paced around the study desk as Miss Calendar looked on. Buffy and the others were seated at the table, staring down, miserable and afraid. Buffy felt very far away. She could hardly concentrate on what they were saying.

"And we're absolutely certain that Angel has reverted to his former self?" Giles queried.

"Yeah, we're all certain. Anybody not feeling certain here?" Xander asked very seriously.

"Giles, you wouldn't have believed him. He was so . . ." Willow took a breath as it all sank in. "He came here to kill us."

Cordelia grimaced at Willow. "What are we going to do?"

"I'm leaning toward blind panic, myself," Giles muttered.

Miss Calendar frowned at him. "Rupert, don't talk like that. The kids."

"I'm sorry." He struggled to compose himself and rubbed his forehead. "It's just, things are bad enough with the Judge here. Angel crossing over to the other side . . . I just wasn't prepared for that."

Miss Calendar murmured, "None of us were."

Buffy held her claddagh ring and slowly turned it in her hand. Across the table, Willow rose and came over to her.

She gently asked, "Are you okay?"

Buffy shook her head.

"Is there anything I can do?" Willow tried.

Again Buffy shook her head. "I should have known," she said mournfully. Tears streaked her face. "I saw him at the house. He was . . . different. The things he said . . ." She couldn't continue.

Giles leaned forward, ready to take notes. "What things?"

Buffy looked away. "It's private."

"But you didn't know he had turned bad?" Miss Calendar asked her.

Willow looked from Buffy to the teacher. "How did you?"

"What?" Miss Calendar said.

"You knew," Willow said slowly. "You told me to get away from him."

Miss Calendar shrugged. "Well, I saw his face."

Giles was still analyzing. "If we only knew how it happened."

That caught Buffy's attention. "What do you mean?" she asked, looking at him as he sat at the table.

"Well, something set it off," he explained. "Some event must have triggered his transformation. If anyone would know, Buffy, it should be you."

Oh, God. Oh, God, no. Please, no.

"I don't," she blurted. "I—"

"Well, did anything happen last night that—"

"Giles, please," she said, distraught, "I can't . . ."

Blindly, she got up and ran out of the room.

"Buffy, I'm sorry, but we can't afford to . . . Buffy!" he called after her.

Willow's gaze locked on Buffy's retreating back as she realized what had happened. What had triggered the transformation. She *knew*.

"Giles, shut up," she said levelly, watching Buffy retreat through the swinging doors.

"This is great." Cordelia counted their many anti-blessings on her fingers. "There's an unkillable demon in town; Angel's joined his team; the Slayer is a basket case. I'd say we've hit bottom."

"I have a plan," Xander announced.

"Oh, no," she chirped sarcastically. "Here's a lower place."

Xander continued, perching on the desk beside Cordelia. "I don't know what's up with Angel, but I may have a way to deal with this Judge guy."

"What do we do?" Willow asked.

He took a breath. He didn't want to widen the chasm between them, but as Willow herself had said, there were more important things to deal with now. He had to be honest, and he had to get everybody to move forward.

"I think I may need Cordelia for this one." A look

passed between him and Willow, and he knew he had hurt her again. *Oh, Will, forgive me someday.* "And we'll need wheels."

Cordelia shrugged. "Well, my car is—"

"It might need to be bigger." Xander looked again at Willow.

She was steely-eyed. "No problem. I'll get Oz. He has a van."

That information—and the harsh way she delivered it—was not lost on Xander. It wasn't that he had a van; it was what they could do inside a van. She was putting him on notice that she was moving on. It felt awful that she felt the need—and, he had to admit, he also felt somewhat jealous—but he had to ignore it for now.

"Good," he said to Willow, silently thanking her. "Okay."

"Care to let me in on the plan that I'm a part of?" Cordelia asked.

Xander shook his head. "No."

"Why not?" She got out of her chair.

Willow rolled her eyes at their typical bickering, which was also not lost on Xander. But he said to Cordy, " 'Cause if I tell you what it is, you won't do it. Just meet me at Willow's in half an hour. And wear something trashy—" He gave her a once-over, "—er."

Insulted, Cordelia opened her mouth in protest and followed him out.

"I'm not sure what we should do about Buffy," Giles mused.

Miss Calendar spoke up. "Assuming they don't attack tonight, I think we should let her be."

Willow glanced at Miss Calendar. "I agree."

"I can imagine what she's going through," Giles said sympathetically.

"No," Willow countered, "I don't think you can."

I gotta crow . . .

Angelus was counting coup, telling his story, savoring his victory. Cradling her doll, Miss Edith, Dru hung on every word. "You should have seen her face. It was priceless."

He hopped up on the storage table and sat on the shelving. "I'll never forget it." In sheer contentment, he crossed his legs at the ankles and sat back.

"So, you didn't kill her then?" Spike sounded less than thrilled.

"Of course not," Angelus shot back, not loving Spike's attitude.

"I know you haven't been in the game for a while, mate, but we do still kill people. It's sort of our *raison d'être,* you know." He spoke as if he were talking to a moron.

"You don't want to kill her, do you," Dru guessed. She extended her two fingers and rammed them into Miss Edith's eyes. The doll, gagged, did not appear to mind. "You want to hurt her. Just like you hurt me." She grinned brilliantly at him.

"Nobody knows me like you do, Dru," he said warmly, laying it on thick for Spike's benefit.

"She'd better not get in our way," Spike said firmly, bringing the conversation back to the present.

Angelus waved his hand. "Don't worry about it."

Spike was giving no quarter. "I do."

"Spike." Angelus flared. He slammed his hand down on a large wooden box. "My boy." Sent the box sliding down the shelving. "You really don't get it, do you?" He stood up, gestured toward Spike in his chair, and laughed at the skinny, white-haired vamp. "You tried to kill her and you couldn't. Look at you. You're a wreck. She's stronger than any Slayer you've ever faced."

He hopped down a step, toward Spike. "Force," he explained, "won't get it done. You gotta work from the inside. To kill this girl," he leaned forward in delicious anticipation, "you have to love her."

Buffy moved quietly into her room and shut the door. She walked to her dressing table, tears still welling, as she touched the silver cross Angel had given her when they had first met. It had become a cherished gift. Now it was a source of protection.

From him.

Trembling, she let go of it, walking away, blinking back the tears, twisting her ring.

She looked down.

It was the ring he had given her.

The tears started spilling down her cheeks as she slipped it from her finger; by the time it was off, the tears were streaming down her face. She carried the claddagh ring to the bed and lay on her coverlet, her resolve crumbling, grief-stricken. She sobbed into her pillow, more alone than she had ever been in her entire life.

* * *

The crimson sheets undulated; silk and satin, smooth, melting like warm candle wax. Angel's hand stroked Buffy's hair, his lips trailed along her skin, his lips found her closed eyes, the side of her nose, her earlobe.

Her fingertips traced his tattoo; her ring glinted against his flesh; his ring gleamed as he rang a finger down her chin. Their sighs mingled, their moans deep with longing. Muscles tightening, hearts pounded . . . the fires of their passion rose, and yet he was so gentle for her, so careful for her.

Angel, oh, my Angel . . .

"I love you," he whispered.

Then Angelus the demon roared at her—

And walked toward her in a daylit cemetery, where she stood with other mourners before an open grave.

Angel looked straight at her and said, "You have to know what to see."

Bewildered, she looked at him, then slowly swung her gaze to the veiled woman beside her. Dressed all in black, Jenny Calendar pulled her veil over her head and stared with sad eyes at the grave.

Buffy opened her eyes.

She had been dreaming.

And this dream meant something.

She was dressed in black. She was on a mission.

Buffy marched to Sunnydale High, completely ignoring the students milling around her. Without missing a beat, she strode into the main building, down the corridor, and into Miss Calendar's computer science classroom.

Students were taking their seats. The teacher was chatting softly with Giles. Buffy brushed past her Watcher, as he said, in mild surprise, "Buffy . . ."

In one swift motion, she grabbed Miss Calendar around the neck and slammed her back onto the desk. Pencils and diskettes flew everywhere.

"Buffy!" Giles cried, grabbing at her arm. Buffy completely ignored him, a calm, deadly purpose in her eyes as she glared at Miss Calendar.

"What do you know?"

As the students looked on in shock, one of them took off his earphones, half-rising as he called out, "Should I get the principal?"

Giles glanced at him. "No. I'll handle this."

Buffy let go of Miss Calendar, allowing her up as she backed away, but pinned her with an unrelenting stare.

"You're all dismissed," Giles said to the class.

As the kids filed out, Buffy never took her eyes off Miss Calendar. "Did you do it? Did you change him?"

Miss Calendar was catching her breath, and did not speak.

"For God's sake, calm down," Giles ordered Buffy.

She ignored him. "Did you know what was going to happen?"

"Buffy, you can't just go accusing people around you of—"

"I didn't know . . . exactly," Miss Calendar said.

That caught Giles's attention. He stood stunned beside Buffy, who waited for Miss Calendar to spill the rest of it.

Miss Calendar looked to Giles first, maybe because she couldn't face Buffy.

"I was told . . ." Then she ticked her glance at Buffy and looked away, murmuring, "Oh, God," under her breath.

Buffy didn't let up.

Miss Calendar took a deep breath and met Buffy's eyes. "I was sent here to watch you. They told me to keep you and Angel apart." She rushed on, shaking her head slightly, "They never told me what would happen."

Giles was stunned. "Jenny—"

"I'm sorry, Rupert." She looked down again, as if she didn't quite believe what she said next. "Angel was supposed to pay for what he did to my people."

"And me?" Buffy demanded. "What was I supposed to be paying for?"

Guilt splashed across Miss Calendar's features. "I didn't know what would happen until after. I swear I would have told you."

The two women were silent for a moment. A silent understanding passed between them.

"So it *was* me," Buffy whispered. "I did it."

"I think so," the teacher said sadly. "I mean, if you—"

Giles stepped forward. "I don't understand."

"The curse," Miss Calendar said to him, rising. "If Angel achieved true happiness, even just a moment of it," she glanced at Buffy, "he would lose his soul."

"But how do you know *you* were responsible?" Giles asked Buffy.

Buffy glanced up at him. Something in her look must

have communicated itself to him. "Oh." Looking uncomfortable in the extreme, he took off his glasses. Buffy was humiliated.

Miss Calendar began, "If there's anything—"

"Curse him again," Buffy said at once.

The teacher shook her head. "No. I can't. Those magicks are long lost, even to my people."

Buffy didn't believe her. "You did it once. It might not be too late to save him."

"It can't be done," Miss Calendar repeated. "I can't help you."

Without hesitation, Buffy said, "Then take me to someone who can."

The smoke from Enyos's pipe wreathed his head as the door to his flat opened. He smiled grimly. He had been waiting for Janna and the young Slayer to arrive.

"I knew she would bring you. I suppose you want answers," he said.

"Not really."

Enyos the Gypsy jumped to his feet and whirled around.

The evil one, Angelus, stood before him in all his vile glory.

"But thanks for the offer," the vampire said.

Oz's van was in the shop, so they had had to wait until tonight to implement Xander's plan. The tension had mounted all day, and finally, they deployed.

It was a dark and stormy night. Oz's van pulled up to

the curb just outside the armory. Willow was in front across from Oz. Xander, in casual clothes and a corduroy jacket, sat in the back next to Cordelia.

Xander said to Willow and Oz, "Wait here. When you guys see that window open, get out the ladder, come up, and we'll pass you the package. Okay?"

"Okay," Oz said calmly.

"Be careful," Willow added.

Xander and Cordelia got out. In her vision of trashier, she wore a metallic headband, large, loud earrings, and a silvery jacket. Also, nice, tight black pants and black gloves, which Xander found kinda kinky.

Xander cut a swath in the chain-link fence that bordered the street. He pulled it back and ducked under easily. Cordelia followed after.

"Security here is really a joke. I really should report it."

"Who am I supposed to be again?" Cordelia asked nervously.

"You're supposed to be a girl. Think you can handle it?"

She smacked him.

"Halt!" someone ordered. Xander and Cordy froze and raised their arms. "Identify yourself right the hell now."

Xander tried not to stammer. "Private Harris, with the, uh, Thirty-third."

"Thirty-third is on maneuvers," the guard said suspiciously.

Uh-oh. "Right. I'm on leave." He and Cordy turned around. "From them." The guard had on cammies and rain gear, and his rifle was pointed straight up in the air.

"You always spend your leave snooping around the armory, buddy?" The guy was trying to sound tough. He was good at it. "And who is she?"

"Hi. I'm not a soldier," Cordelia said brightly. She looked at Xander. "Right?"

Xander walked up to the guy, a little more up close and personal. "Look, I just want to give her the tour. You know what I'm saying?"

The soldier wasn't getting it. "The tour?"

Xander moved into man-to-man mode. "Well, you know the ladies. They love to see the big guns. Gets 'em all hot and bothered. Can you cut me some slack, give me a blind eye?"

"And why should I?" tough guy asked.

"Well, if you do, I won't tell Colonel Newsome that your shoes ain't regulation, your post wasn't covered, and you hold your gun like a sissy girl."

While he was talking, Xander grabbed his rifle and thrust it into the guy's hands the way he was supposed to hold it, across his chest.

The threat worked. The guard said, "You got twenty minutes, nimrod."

"I just need five," Xander assured him. Then he thought better of that. "Uh, forget I said that last part."

He opened the brown door marked Secured Area for Cordelia.

On the other side, they wandered in dim light among dozens of weapons of all shapes and sizes.

"Okay, what was that?" Cordelia asked. "And who are you?"

Xander closed and locked the door. "Remember Halloween? I got turned into a soldier?"

"Yeah."

"Well, I still remember all of it. I know procedure, ordnance, access codes, everything. I know the whole layout for this base and I'm pretty sure I can put together an M16 in fifty-seven seconds."

"Well, I'm sort of impressed," she conceded, smiling. "But let's just find the thing and get out of here."

"Okay."

She sat on a crate. "So looking at guns makes girls want to have sex? That's scary."

"Yeah, I guess." Xander scrutinized the supplies.

"Well, does looking at guns make *you* want to have sex?"

"I'm seventeen," he said flatly. "Looking at linoleum makes me want to have sex."

Willow was anxious. "I wish they'd hurry."

Oz was curious. "So, do you guys steal weapons from the army a lot?"

"Well, we don't have cable, so we have to make our own fun, " she told him.

"I get you." He smiled faintly.

Suddenly, she blurted, "Do you want to make out with me?"

"What?" He was a bit taken aback.

"Forget it. I'm sorry." She looked away, embarrassed. Then she looked back at him. "Well, do you?"

He thought about his answer. Then he said, "Sometimes when I'm sitting in class, you know, I'm not thinking about class, 'cause that would never happen. I think about kissing you and then it's like, everything stops. It's like, freeze frame. Willow kissage."

She glowed.

"Oh, I'm not going to kiss you," he added.

"What? But freeze frame—" she protested.

"Well, to the casual observer, it would appear you want to make your friend Xander jealous. Or even the score, or something. That's on the empty side. See, in my fantasy, when I'm kissing you, you're kissing me."

He paused. "It's okay. I can wait." She looked charmed, with her fuzzy-collar coat and her sweet little dangling earrings, and he was glad. All he had wanted was to be honest, but this girl was worth a lot of effort. If in addition, she found something else to like about him, that was on the plus side.

"We're up," he told her, as the window opened.

Miss Calendar led the way into her uncle's room, followed by Buffy, and then Giles.

Miss Calendar saw the body first, and gasped, "Oh, my God."

Buffy stared, and Giles almost lost it. His hand hovered near his mouth.

Then they saw the message on the wall, written in blood, and in Angelus's handwriting: *Was it good for you too?*

"He's doing this deliberately, Buffy. He's trying to

make it harder for you." Giles said, obviously trying to soothe her.

She kept her eyes fixed on the words. On the cruelty. "He's only making it easier. I know what I have to do."

Giles looked at her. "What?"

"Kill him," she said simply.

CHAPTER 4

At the factory, the Judge was all duded up in a coarse brown robe. Angelus wished he'd thought to buy the big guy a corsage.

"I am ready," the demon intoned.

" 'Bout time," Spike grumbled.

Dru sat on his lap and made sorry-you-can't-come little moans as she tenderly kissed him goodbye. He sat stoically, "Have a good time."

"Too bad you can't come with," Angelus whispered in his ear. He patted his arm. "We'll be thinking of you."

"I won't be in this chair forever." It was a bit of threat. Angelus repaid him for it by lifting Dru's hand away from Spike's face and possessively grasping it.

Spike attempted a tit-for-tat, which Angelus found less than impressive. "What happens if your girlfriend shows up?"

"I'm going to give her a kiss," Angelus said breezily.

He came up next to the Judge, while Dru looked over her shoulder at Spike.

"Don't you look spiffy," Angelus said merrily.

The Judge muttered, "Spiffy?"

In Giles's office, Xander and Oz deposited an oblong wooden crate on his desk. Back in the library, Cordelia and Willow were loading weapons into a gym bag.

"Happy Birthday, Buffy," Xander said. "I hope you like the color."

Buffy stepped forward, observing while Giles took a crowbar to the lid.

"Giles, we'll hit the factory first, but we may not find them. If they're on the offensive, we need to figure out where they'll go," Buffy strategized. Adrenaline was coursing through her. She was ready to fight.

"Agreed," Giles said, prying open the lid. He threw it back.

Buffy gazed at the contents. "This is good."

Hovering in the doorway, Miss Calendar took an uncertain step forward. "Do you . . ." she asked tentatively, "is there something I can do to—"

Buffy didn't even look at her. All she said was, "Get out."

Giles looked across the room at the teacher, as she said softly, "I just want to help."

Giles looked down slightly, then turned his back. "She said get out." No joy there, no anger. Just siding with his Slayer, that was all. But Buffy scrutinized him, both touched and saddened that he had been forced to pick sides. That any of this had happened.

Miss Calendar withdrew. Xander approached, and asked Buffy, "Do you want me to show you how to use it?"

"Yes, I do." She was all business, and no heart. *I don't know if I'll ever have a heart again.*

I hope not.

Then they went to the factory.

It was deserted, the party favors gone, the high-backed chairs stripped of flowers and vines.

"I knew it," Buffy huffed in frustration.

Giles looked around. "And we haven't a bead on where they would go?"

"I don't know," she answered.

No one noticed the vampire in the wheelchair, lurking in the shadows, and Spike was determined to keep it that way.

"Somewhere crowded, I guess. I mean, the Judge needs bodies, right?" She joined Xander, Cordy, and Willow, preparing to go.

"The Bronze?" Willow suggested.

"It's closed tonight," Xander told her.

"There's not a lot of choices in Sunnydale," Cordelia pointed out. "It's not like people are going to line up to get massacred."

Oz spoke up. "Uh, guys? If I were going to line up, I know where I'd go."

The Sunnydale Mall.

More specifically, the mall multiplex.

And here they are, Angelus thought, very pleased as he, Dru, and their minions escorted the Judge to the upper level. *All the walking, talking battery chargers my Eveready guy needs.*

As if on cue, an oblivious businessman carrying a briefcase walked up the stairs, directly into the Judge's line of fire. The Judge stretched out his left hand, shooting energy at the man. The man began to burn, just as Dalton had. Fire blazed from his eye sockets, and then the flames flared out from inside his body. Within seconds, he was entirely consumed.

Satisfied, Angelus said to his minions, "Lock the exits, boys." And to the Judge, "It's all yours."

The Judge looked pretty darn happy about that.

The elevator doors opened, and Buffy led the way. Giles came up behind her, the oblong box on his shoulder.

"Everybody keep back. Damage control only," she ordered, as they marched down the mall. "Take out any lesser vamps if you can. I'll handle the Smurf."

The Judge took up position on the stairway, flanked by Angelus and the lovely Dru. Not so surprisingly—to Angelus, anyway, because he had lived among the cattle—the shoppers continued on their way, no one having noticed the annihilation of the businessman. *Ants,* Angelus thought derisively, *half-witted blood bags.*

The Judge opened wide his arms. Fiery pulses emanated from him, connecting to the humans closest to him, then shooting directly through them to others, and to others. It was a connect-the-dots web of energy. The Judge was loving it. Angelus was loving that he loved it.

Dru bounced on her heels and cooed, "Oh, goody."

Then someone shot an arrow directly into the Judge's chest. He winced, stumbling backward, which turned off his power. The people he had attacked staggered and gasped, but for the most part, were alive.

He pulled the arrow from his chest, breaking it off in the process.

"Who dares?" he bellowed.

Angelus turned, his eyes wide.

Buffy kept her position on top of the popcorn machine. She was about fifty yards away from the Judge, who was standing at the top of a double set of stairs. As Buffy had expected, Angelus and Dru were with him.

"I think I got his attention," she said with grim satisfaction.

The Judge addressed her directly. "You are a fool. No weapon forged can stop me."

"That was then." She handed Xander the crossbow. "This is now."

She took the rocket launcher from Giles.

She put it on her shoulder, and aimed. It made a whining noise as it armed itself. The shoppers started screaming and scattering.

She flicked the switch, took aim.

Across the building, Angelus looked at Dru, and she at him. They both knew what was up.

Hurtling themselves forward, they abandoned the Judge, who asked, with mild curiosity and a touch of concern, "What's *that* do?"

Angelus and Dru leaped over the stairway balcony as Buffy pulled the trigger. The package screamed straight for the Judge, made impact, and blew him to bits. His vampire companions were thrown forward by the blast. Drusilla and Angelus both landed hard, as tiny fragments of the Judge rained down on them like a scattershot of rock.

Angelus got to his feet and disappeared. Dru was left behind, completely wigging out, scurrying away in a paroxysm of whimpering. Her henchmen trailed after her.

Buffy took a moment to register the kill as smoke from the blast billowed toward the ceiling. The others peeked from behind the concession stand.

"My best present ever," she said to Xander, handing him the rocket launcher.

Xander took it from her. "Knew you'd like it."

"Do you think he's dead?" Willow asked.

"We can't be sure," Buffy answered. "Pick up the pieces. Keep them separate."

The others moved to obey. But Cordelia grumbled, "Pieces? We're getting *pieces?* Our job sucks!"

Buffy ignored her. Her job was not finished.

It had barely begun.

Angelus ran.

Then he saw the Slayer staring after him, and ran faster. He threw people out of his way in an effort to get the hell out of there.

Buffy jumped off the popcorn machine in hot pursuit.

Meanwhile, the burning debris of the Judge created a lot of smoke. The smoke set off the overhead sprinklers.

Soon the interior of the mall was soaking with water with more cascading down.

Then there she was, confined in a cul-de-sac containing a pastry counter and little else, searching for him. Angelus seized the advantage and attacked her from behind. She went down, and he thought, *Maybe this will be easier than I expected.*

"You know what the worst part was?" he asked roughly, glaring at her through the sprinkler downpour as she got to her knees and faced him. "Pretending that I loved you. If I'd known how easily you'd give it up, I wouldn't have even bothered."

She got to her feet and gave him that sad, mad look of hers. He knew she was fury in a bottle. *Oh, I know this Slayer, inside and out.*

"That doesn't work anymore," she said coldly. "You're not Angel."

"You'd like to think that, wouldn't you? Doesn't matter." He grinned at her, savoring her pain. "The important thing is, you made me the man I am today."

That got her. She kicked him in the face, then punched his arm. He did her one better and belted her in the face, then the stomach, grabbing her head and whirling around, laying her out with a sharp side kick to the head.

She went down again.

They were picking up the pieces, the Scoobs, when Oz stopped, raised his hand, and pointed at quite a large part, not quite daring to touch it.

"Uh, arm," he announced.

* * *

In the mall cul-de-sac, Angelus was gaining the upper hand. As Buffy leaped to her feet, he picked her up over his shoulder and flung her back down to the floor. She sprang back up, but he blocked her blow and got in a sharp undercut to her chin, whipping back her head. Then a left, and then a right.

And then she was down again.

"Not quitting on me already, are you?" he said, reveling in the fear on her face. *Those enormous eyes are so expressive. They tell me everything I need to know. She's tired, and she's scared. Just the way I love her best.*

"Come on, Buffy," he sneered. "You know you want it, huh?"

The fear galvanized into anger. She flung herself at him, and the kicks and punches came so fast and furious he couldn't keep count of how many times she'd connected. She used him like a punching bag, and then she dragged him forward, ramming his head through a glass case, then back up through the glass top. She pummeled him. A front kick, a roundhouse. He was thrown backward and landed on the floor.

When he jumped up, she had a stake in her hand.

They looked at each other.

He saw her waver. Her face was a study in pain.

He smiled as she lowered her arm.

"You can't do it," he said triumphantly. "You can't kill me."

Her pain hardened into anger. Before he realized what she was doing, she kicked him with all her Slayer's strength right between the legs.

He groaned and doubled over, mouth open in a silent

scream of pain. He couldn't make another sound as he gagged and fell to his knees.

Buffy turned her back and walked away in the water-sprinkler rain.

She said, almost too softly for him to hear, "Give me time."

Giles drove her home. They sat in front of her house in his Citröen, and she was so ashamed she couldn't even look at him.

She could feel him looking at her, but she stared straight ahead. He turned off the rattling motor and said, not without kindness, "It's not over. I suppose you know that."

She nodded slightly, and looked down.

"He'll come after *you,* particularly. His profile—well, he's likely to strike out at the things that made him the most human."

In a hoarse, tight voice, she rasped, "You must be so disappointed in me." Finally, she looked at him.

"No. No, I'm not," he said sincerely.

"But this is all my fault." Tears welled. *Giles, I'm so miserable,* she wanted to say. *I almost wish I'd died.*

He turned in his seat and shook his head. "I don't believe it is. Do you want me to wag my finger at you and tell you you acted rashly? You did, and I can."

She looked down, preparing herself for words that she knew would hurt.

"But I know that you loved him, and he has proven more than once that he loved you."

She glanced back at him, hungry for forgiveness, starving for his gentle words of comfort. "You couldn't have known what would happen. The coming months are going to be hard, I suspect, on all of us. But if it's guilt you're looking for, Buffy, I'm not your man. All you will get from me is my support and my respect."

Her silence spanned the space between them.

Her tears ran like rain.

Her mother had told her that the actor's name was Robert Young. Buffy couldn't remember the name of the actress who was singing, *"Good night, my love. My moment with you now is ending."* They were rich people on a luxurious cruise on a vast ocean of black and white.

Buffy's mom came in with a cup of coffee and a plate with two bakery cupcakes on it. One was topped with an unlit candle.

She brought them over to the coffee table and sat beside Buffy on the couch. They were similarly dressed, Joyce in an oversized sweater, leggings, and socks, and Buffy in a large gray V-neck top, white cargo pants, and a pair of her mother's socks.

Joyce glanced at the TV and asked, "Did I miss anything?"

Buffy roused herself. "Oh, uh, just some singing. And some running around."

Her mom looked inside a wooden box and a round pottery bowl with a lid, and finally located a book of matches. "I'm sorry I didn't have time to make you a real cake."

"No. This is good." She meant it. *This is home. My mother. The life I don't usually have.*

"But we're still going shopping tomorrow. So what'd you do for your birthday? Did you have fun?"

Buffy's throat tightened. *Oh, Mom, Mom, I so want to tell you. I so need you. I need.*

"I got older."

Her mother looked mildly surprised at the sadness in her voice. "You look the same to me." Her love for Buffy was in her eyes, and in her smile.

Then she lit the candle on the cupcake. "Happy birthday." She made a face and begged theatrically, "I don't have to sing, do I?"

Buffy tried to smile. "No."

"Well, go on," her mother urged. "Make a wish."

Buffy looked at the tiny point of light.

"I'll just let it burn."

She laid her head on her mother's chest. Joyce stroked her hair thoughtfully.

The black and white people sang, *"Good night, my love."*

And Buffy watched the candle burn.

THE THIRD CHRONICLE:

Passion

PROLOGUE

The Bronze. It was the same as it had always been. Through the weeks and months since his change, he had wondered if anything would ever be different in the Slayer's little circle. Granted, Xander and Cordelia had become an official couple. The little sweetheart, Willow, was dating Oz, the guitarist.

Love. How mundane.

Then he realized that *he* could make changes. In fact, he was already in the process of changing everything.

Always at the apex, that's me.

Angelus stood on the balcony and looked down on the dancers. The sensual rhythm of the music stirred seductive movements, glances; the candlelight from the glass votives on the tables caught the warmth and glow on their faces. Languid smiles passed; questions were asked, promises made.

Angelus moved down the stairway, searching. He knew she was there. He could smell her; feel her.

He stared through the crowd. She was dancing. Smiling. In a tight T-strap top and skirt, her hair tousled as if from savage kissing, she swayed and rolled her hips. Her eyes were on her friend, Xander, as he danced with her. The young man was not unaffected, but it was clear that he knew this was a moment between friends, not lovers. Cordelia, assured of her changed status as his official girlfriend, chatted easily with Willow at a table on the perimeter.

Angelus watched. He stared, unblinking. His gaze devoured every gesture. He walked around the edge of the dance floor, never blinking, moving fluidly, a hungry, intent predator.

Passion, he thought. *It lies in all of us. Sleeping, waiting, and though unwanted, unbidden, it will stir, open its jaws, and howl.*

She was wearing vanilla, her new scent. She had worn it on the night they had made love. It wafted through the night air as she left with her friends, arm in arm with Willow, Xander and Cordelia bringing up the rear. As they passed him, he inhaled the aroma, drinking the blood of the victim in his arms, a young woman he embraced as if she were his lover, when all she was was food.

The four were innocent, unaware as they chatted, Willow sucking a Tootsie Roll pop with girlish casualness. Still in vamp face, Angelus let the young woman's body drop to the ground as the Slayer's group strolled on . . .

He morphed back to his human face and trailed them.

One by one, her friends left Buffy's side, to go home to their beds. At last, she was alone, in her room. The window was open, and though she peered through the Venetian blinds as though she sensed something, she left all the lights on as she undressed and got ready for bed. Another might see a beautiful school-age girl setting her alarm clock and climbing into bed. Lying back into the darkness in pink satin, closing her eyes. Angelus saw the Slayer, an exquisite, highly dangerous creature of unbelievable power.

He remembered her touch.

Her trust.

He crept in through the window and sat on her bed. Studied her as she slept. The pulse in her neck beat rapidly. Perhaps she was dreaming of him. Gently, he smoothed a tendril of hair from her face, trailing his fingertips against her forehead, her temple, and inhaled her scent.

It speaks to us, guides us. Passion rules us all, and we obey. What other choice do we have?

CHAPTER 1

Brilliant sunlight streamed through Buffy's window as she slowly woke. To the pleasant chirping of birds, she turned her head and stretched, opening her eyes.

A brown parchment envelope lay on her pillow. She sat up as she opened it, unfolding a thick piece of matching stationery.

It was a charcoal sketch of her, her eyes closed in peaceful, unsuspecting slumber.

Left on my pillow. For me to find.
For me to know.

Dressed in an animal print velour, a small white backpack slung over her shoulders, Buffy burst into the school library. Giles was stamping books, of all things, and Cordelia, fashionable in a blue chambray shirt and a gray skirt, was chatting with Xander, who was perched on the back of one of the wooden chairs.

Buffy said tersely, "He was in my room."

Giles looked up from his task and asked politely, "Who?"

She stomped over to the study table. "Angel. He was in my room last night."

Cordelia and Xander looked shocked. His rubber stamp in his hand, Giles moved from behind the circulation desk through his office, to join Buffy at the table.

"Are you sure?" he said, clearly astonished.

"Positive," she assured him. "When I woke up, I found a picture he'd left me on my pillow."

Xander piped up. "A visit from the pointed-tooth fairy."

Cordelia frowned. "Wait. I thought vampires couldn't come in unless you invited them in."

Giles turned to her. "Yes, but if you invite them in once, thereafter, they are always welcome."

"You know, I think there may be a valuable lesson for you gals here about inviting strange men into your bedrooms." Xander wasn't joking.

"Oh, God! I invited him in my car once," Cordelia realized. "That means he could come back into my car whenever he wants!"

Xander wore a regretful expression. "Yep. You're doomed to having to give him and his vamp pals a lift whenever they feel like it. And those guys *never* chip in for gas."

"Giles, there has to be some sort of spell to reverse the invitation, right?" Buffy insisted. She was wigged and she didn't care who knew it. "Like a barrier—'no shoes, no pulse, no service' kind of thing?"

"Yeah, that works for a car, too?" Cordelia chimed in.

Giles was already in motion. "Yes. Well, I could check my—"

Xander stood as two underclassmen types wandered into the library. "Hel-*lo*," he said gruffly. "Excuse me, but have you ever heard of knocking?"

One was a boy, the other a redheaded girl. The boy said, a little defensively, "We're supposed to get some books. On Stalin."

Xander pointed an accusing finger at them. "Does this look like a Barnes and Noble?"

"This *is* the school library, Xander," Giles reproved quietly.

"Since when?" Xander asked, as if this was news to him.

Giles took over. "Yes. Third row, historical biographies."

"Thanks," the boy said.

He and the girl student walked past the silent group and went up the stairs to the second level.

Xander gestured for the group to ogay into the allway-bay. Together they tiptoed out, just as the boy student emerged from the stacks and said, "Uh, did you say that was . . . Hello?"

They walked down the corridor and out into the sunshine. Giles resumed. "So, Angel has decided to step up his harassment of you."

"By sneaking into her room and leaving stuff at night?" Cordelia said bluntly. "Why doesn't he just slit her throat or strangle her in her sleep or cut her heart out?" At a disbelieving, ironic grin from Xander, she held out her arms and said, "What? I'm trying to help."

"Yes." Giles spoke directly to Buffy. "It's classic battle strategy, to throw one's opponent off his game. He's *trying* to provoke you. To taunt you, to goad you into some mishap or something of that sort."

"The 'nyah, nyah, nyah, nyah' approach to battle," Xander, the soul of helpfulness, explained.

"Yes, Xander," Giles said, with the tiniest, most British bit of sarcasm, "once again you've managed to boil a complex thought down to its simplest possible form."

Buffy was having nothing to do with banter mode. This was deadly serious stuff. "Giles, Angel once told me that when he was obsessed with Drusilla, the first thing he did was to kill her family."

Xander got it at once. "Your mom."

"I know. I'm going to have to tell her something. The truth?" She turned and looked at Giles.

He shook his head in deadly earnest. "No. You can't do that."

"Yeah. The more people who know the secret, the more it cheapens it for the rest of us," Xander riffed, as Cordelia rolled her eyes.

"I've got to tell her something," Buffy said urgently. "I have to *do* something. Giles, Angel has an all-access pass to my house and I'm not always there when my mother is. I can't protect her."

"I told you, I will find a spell," Giles reminded her.

"What about until you find a spell?" she pushed.

"Until then, you and your mother are welcome to ride around with me in my car," Cordelia said, full of graciousness.

Giles stayed with the topic. "Buffy, I understand your concern, but it is imperative that you keep a level head through all this."

She was frustrated with him. "That's easy for you to say. You don't have Angel lurking in your bedroom at night."

"I know how hard this is for you." She blinked. "All right," he admitted, "I don't. But as the Slayer, you don't have the luxury of being a slave to your passions. You mustn't let Angel get to you, no matter how provocative his behavior may become."

"So what you're basically saying is 'Just ignore him and maybe he'll go away.' " A statement she uttered without conviction or joy.

Giles considered. Then he nodded. "Yes, precisely."

"Hey, how come Buffy doesn't get a snotty 'once again you boil it down to the simplest form' thing?" Xander grumbled. "Watcher's pet," he flung at her.

Jenny Calendar's computer science class was winding up for the day.

"Don't forget I need your sample spreadsheets by the end of the week." Over the peal of the bell, she added, "Oh, and I want both a paper printout and a copy on disk."

As Willow began to leave, Miss Calendar reached out a hand and said, "Willow?"

Willow stopped at her desk. "Yes?"

"I might be a little late tomorrow. Do you think you could cover my class 'til I show?"

Willow was flabbergasted "Really? Me? Teach the class? Sure!"

"Cool," Miss Calendar said offhandedly.

"Oh, wait . . . but what if they don't recognize my authority?" Willow fretted. "What if they try to convince me that you always let them leave class early? What if there's a fire drill?" She escalated. "What if there's a *fire?*"

Holding her coffee cup, Miss Calendar leaned slightly across her desk. "Willow, you're going to be fine. And I'll try not to be too late, okay?"

Willow calmed down. "Okay, good. Earlier is good." She brightened as possibilities opened up. "Will I have the power to assign detention? Or make 'em run laps?"

From the doorway, Buffy said in a strained voice, "Hey, Will."

"Hi, Buffy," Miss Calendar said tentatively. "Rupert."

Giles looked uncomfortable as Buffy ignored Miss Calendar and focused on Willow. "Willow, I thought I might take in a class. Figured I could use someone who knows where they are."

Chagrined, Willow ducked her head and crossed over to Buffy. They left the room together, as Willow murmured, "Sorry. I *have* to talk to her. She's a teacher, and teachers are to be respected. Even if they're only filling in until the real teacher shows up. Otherwise, chaos could ensue and . . ."

* * *

Jenny Calendar wilted at the slight. *Well, I deserve it.* She took a breath, picked up her mail, and began thumbing through it.

Then she realized that Rupert had stayed behind. Now he crossed the threshold and entered her classroom, looking as uncomfortable as she was. It was the first time they had been near each other since he had told her to get out the night Buffy destroyed the Judge.

A little hopeful, a little flustered, she said to him, "How've you been?"

"Not so good, actually," he admitted. "Since Angel lost his soul, he's regained his sense of whimsy."

He's talking to me, she thought, her stomach doing a little flip. *That must mean he forgives me in some small measure.*

She crossed her arms as she took in what he was telling her. "That sounds bad." And it did; her pleasure in being able to talk to him took nothing away from that.

"He's been in Buffy's bedroom. I need to drum up a spell to keep him out of the house."

She reached for a weatherbeaten book on her desk. "This might help." She handed it to him. "I've been doing a little reading since Angel changed." Glancing at the cover, she mused, "I don't think you have that one."

He was obviously touched. "Thank you." He opened it, scanned a bit.

As he perused the book, she tried to strengthen the whisper-thin connection. "So, how's Buffy doing?" Besides, she really cared how Buffy was.

He shut the book, looked down for a moment, and raised his chin. Coolly, he replied, "How do you think?"

They regarded each other for a moment. Then she admitted defeat. Turning away, she said, "I know you feel betrayed."

"Yes, well, that's one of the unpleasant side effects of betrayal," he returned.

"Rupert, I was raised by the people that Angel hurt the most. My duty to them was the first thing I was ever taught. I didn't come here to hurt anyone. And I lied to you because I thought it was the right thing to do."

She looked away. "I didn't know what would happen." Her voice became a whisper. "I didn't know I was going to fall in love with you."

They had gotten to know each other over a year ago, when she had headed a project to scan all the books into the library. Willow Rosenberg, one of her prize students, had accidentally scanned a demon into the net, and Jenny had felt it necessary to blow her cover to the extent of coming forward and identifying herself as a technopagan.

Their relationship had grown from there, and she had never faced the fact that someday she would have to tell him who she was and what she was doing in Sunnydale.

In the ensuing silence, she looked up at him. She couldn't read his expression, and she was humiliated. "Oh, God," she said miserably, "is it too late to take that back?"

"Do you want to?" he asked.

"I just want to be right with you," she said softly. "I don't expect more. I just want so badly to make all this up to you."

"I understand." His tone was kind, if laced with caution. "But I'm not the one you need to make it up to." He smiled gently. "Thank you for the book."

With that, he left.

There was baked chicken, salad, bread, potatoes. Buffy ate none of it.

Finally, Joyce said, "Okay. What's wrong?"

Buffy was caught off guard. "It's . . . nothing."

"Come on, you can tell me anything," Joyce pressed. "I've read all the parenting books. You cannot surprise me."

I sure can, Buffy thought, but that was very beside the point. Her mom was her mom, after all. She was supposed to be able to tell her things.

She took a chance. Laying down her fork, she began. "Do you remember that guy, Angel?"

"Angel? The college boy who was tutoring you in history?" Joyce filled in.

That was what I told you the first time you met him, wasn't it? Buffy thought. *I just conveniently left out the part about how he had just saved my life from three vampire assassins.*

"Right. Well, he . . . I . . . we're sort of dating. *Were* dating." She shrugged and smiled uneasily. "We're going through a serious 'off again' phase right now." *Because he's a demon.*

Her mother gave her a knowing look. "Don't tell me. 'He's changed. He's not the same guy you fell for.' "

Oh, God, why did I even start this? "In a nutshell. Anyway, since he changed, he's been kind of following me around. He's having trouble letting go."

Joyce's face clouded. "Buffy, has he . . . done anything?"

"No, no, it's not like that," Buffy said quickly. *I wish I hadn't started this,* she thought. *I can't tell her what's really going on.* "He's just been hanging around. A lot. Just sending me notes. That kind of thing. I don't want to see him right now. I mean, if he shows up, I'll talk to him." She had to say that to keep her mother from worrying. She tried to toss in casually, "Just don't invite him in."

Seriously, don't invite him in, Mom, she added, like a prayer.

Willow was on the portable phone with Buffy. She was in her PJs, and she was shutting down for the night.

"I agree with Giles," she told Buffy as she moved around her room. "You need to just try and not let him get to you. Angel's only doing this to try to get you to do something stupid. I swear, men can be such jerks sometimes . . . dead or alive." Firmly, she closed her laptop.

On the other end, Buffy admitted, "I just hope Giles can find a 'keep out' spell soon. I know I'll sleep easier when I can . . . sleep easier."

"I'm sure he will," Willow said, sprinkling fish food into her new aquarium. She'd gotten it for Hanukkah. "He's, like, Book Man. Until then, try and keep happy thoughts and . . ."

Willow lost track of what she was saying as she noticed a brown parchment envelope on her colorful block quilt.

"'And what?" Buffy prodded "Willow?"

Willow slowly opened the envelope. There was a

piece of fishing line inside; frowning, she started pulling it out, realizing just at that moment that there were no fish in her aquarium.

Because they were all dead, and hanging from the strand of fishing line in her hand.

A short time later, Willow was at Buffy's. Strings of garlic hung everywhere in Buffy's room and, as the two sat together on Buffy's bed in their pajamas, Willow kept a very tight grip on a very sharp stake.

Her frightened gaze swept the room as she said, "Thanks for having me over, Buffy. Especially on a school night and all."

"No problem," Buffy assured her. "Hey, sorry about your fish."

"It's okay," Willow said sadly. "We hadn't really had time to bond yet." She wrinkled up her face. "Although, for the first time, I'm glad my parents didn't let me have a puppy."

The words hit home. Her eyes downcast, Buffy murmured, "It's so weird. Every time something like this happens my first instinct is to run to Angel. I can't believe it's the same person. He's completely different from the guy that I knew."

"Well, sort of, except . . ." Willow trailed off.

Buffy looked at her. "Except what?"

"You're still the only thing he thinks about."

The two friends looked at each other.

Angelus watched from the shadows as Drusilla swept into the factory with a fluffy little white dog hidden behind her back. She lit up when she saw Spike, who was glowering in his wheelchair.

She carried the whimpering pup over to him, announcing, "I brought something for you."

Spike didn't even look at her.

"Poor thing. She's an orphan. Her owner died . . . without a fight." Dru grinned and slipped her hand into the top of Spike's black T-shirt, bending down beside him. "Do you like her? I brought her especially for you, to cheer you up." She jerked on his T-shirt.

"And I've named her Sunshine." She spoke in the singsong voice mothers used with their little ones.

Still hidden, Angelus chuckled to himself as Spike clenched his jaw, Roller Boy's irritation obviously mounting.

"Open wide," Dru encouraged Spike. He turned his head. "Come on, love," she cajoled him. "You need to eat something to keep your strength up. Now . . ." She waved the dog like an airplane headed for the hangar and made little growling noises. "Open up for Mummy . . ."

"I won't have you feeding me like a child, Dru!" he snapped, pushing his wheelchair away from her.

That's my cue, Angelus thought, sauntering from the shadows. "Why not?" he asked Spike. "She already bathes you, carries you around, and changes you like a child." He smiled at Dru.

Ouch. If looks could kill, I'd be dust, Angelus thought gleefully as Spike glared at him.

"My Angel! Where have you been?" Dru demanded,

her voice petulant and inviting. "The sun is almost up, and it can be so hurtful. We were worried."

"No, we weren't," Spike said darkly, levelly meeting Angelus's gaze.

"You must forgive Spike. He's just a bit testy tonight. Doesn't get out much anymore." Dru looked pityingly at her white-haired boyfriend.

Angelus leaned forward, determined to needle Spike as much as possible. It was almost too easy, but one took one's pleasure where it appeared . . .

"Well, maybe next time I'll bring you with me, Spike." Angelus matched his glare and raised it a few degrees of contempt. "Might be handy to have you along if I ever need a really good parking space."

Spike was starting to simmer. "Have you forgotten that you're a bloody guest in my bloody home?"

"And as a guest," Angelus said with mock solicitousness, "if there's anything I can do for you . . . Any responsibility I can assume while you're spinning your wheels . . . Anything I'm not *already* doing, that is." He leered at Dru.

"That's *enough!*" Spike shouted. He pushed Angelus out of his face.

Angelus started laughing. *He's so easy. I can play him like a violin.*

"Awww," Dru cooed. She kissed Spike on the cheek and put Sunshine in his lap. His gaze never left Angelus as she walked away, stroking her own cheek. "You two boys . . . fighting over me and all." She chuckled and stopped by the dining table, trailing her fingers down the center of her bodice. "Makes a girl feel . . ."

Then she trailed off, her words giving way to a frightened, childlike cry. Holding out her left hand, she began to breathe hard, as if she were in pain.

"Dru? What is it, pet?" Spike asked, alert.

She gazed into a place only she could see. "The air . . . it worries. Someone . . . an old enemy, is seeking help to destroy our happy home."

Moaning, near tears, she clutched one of the chairs for support. Otherwise she would have sunk to the floor.

The brass bells hanging over the door to the Dragon's Cove magic store tinkled as Jenny Calendar entered and looked around. The store was filled with beads, suncatchers, and bottles of murky liquids containing fetal pigs, curiosities, and monstrosities. Black candles burned, glowing scarlet, and spicy incense permeated the air.

"Welcome," the balding store clerk said. Looking and sounding vaguely Middle Eastern, he wore a white shirt and pants, an amulet, and strings of yellow beads around his neck. "How may I serve you today? Love potion? Perhaps a voodoo doll for that unfaithful—"

Cutting him off, she said, "I need an orb of Thesulah."

Immediately he dropped his act. "Oh, you're in the trade." His accent disappeared, too. "Follow me. Sorry about the spiel, but around Valentine's Day, I get a lot of tourists shopping for love potions and mystical revenge on past lovers." He shrugged philosophically. "Sad fact is, Ouija boards and rabbits' feet—that's what pays the rent here."

He went behind a case of white china decanters filled with herbs, pulled back the curtain to a spacious pantry, and started searching the shelves. "So, how'd you hear about us?"

Idly she examined a display of crystals and rune-stones. "My uncle, Enyos, told me about you."

He glanced at her as he picked up a mahogany container. "So you're Janna, then. Sorry to hear about your uncle."

"Thank you."

"He was a good customer," he added frankly. He set the box on the glass counter. "Well, here you go, one Thesulan orb." With a flourish he took the lid off the container, revealing a small, crystal sphere nestled in a blanket of velvet. "Spirit vault for the Rituals of the Undead."

Jenny gave it a quick glance. It was exactly what she wanted. She handed him her credit card as he continued chattering. "I don't get much call for those lately. Sold a couple as 'new age' paperweights last year." He ran the card through the machine. "Yeah, I just love the 'new agers.' They helped send my youngest to college."

His tone became a touch more businesslike as he wrote up the bill of sale. "By the way, you *do* know that the transliteration annals for the Ritual of the Undead were lost. Without the annals, the surviving text is gibberish."

She looked up from signing the receipt. "And without a translated text, the orbs of Thesulah are pretty much useless. I know." She tore off his copy and handed it to him.

"I only mention it because I have a strict policy of no refunds."

"It's okay." She put her copy in her purse and he replaced the lid for her. "I'm working on a computer program to translate the Romanian liturgy to English, based on a random sampling of the text."

He folded his hands on the counter. "Ahh. I don't like computers. They give me the willies."

She picked the container up and cradled it against her chest. "Well, thank you."

She was almost out the door when he called after her, "By the way, not that it's any of my business, really, but what are you planning to conjure up if you can decipher the text?"

She took off the lid and lifted the orb to the sunlight streaming through the window. "A present for a friend of mine."

"Really?" He was interested. "What are you going to give him?"

In her hand, the orb began to glow. It cast a warm glow against her skin and gleamed in her eyes.

Jenny answered simply, "His soul."

CHAPTER 2

Xander caught up with Willow and Buffy as they joined the reluctant morning saunter toward Sunnydale High. He was wearing his wacky plaid pants, and he smiled brightly and said, "Well, good morning, ladies. And what did you two do last night?"

"We had kind of a pajama-party-sleepover-with-weapons thing," Willow informed him.

"Oh," he said rather wistfully. "And I don't suppose either of you had the presence of mind to locate a camera to capture the moment?"

Buffy smiled faintly. Willow was too on purpose to even register a reaction. "I have to go. I have a class to teach in about five minutes and I have to arrive early to glare disapprovingly at the stragglers."

Then her face fell as she spotted Jenny Calendar walking briskly across the lawn in her clunky black heels and wispy dress. "Oh, darn. She's here. Five hours of lesson planning yesterday down the drain."

Willow trudged off. Buffy kept her attention focused on Miss Calendar as she murmured to Xander, "You know what? I'll see you in class." She moved away from him and intercepted Miss Calendar. "Hey."

"Hi." Miss Calendar looked surprised, a little on guard, a little hopeful. "Is there something . . . did you want something?"

Buffy took a breath. "Look, I know you feel badly about what happened and I just want to say . . ." She trailed off. *I can't do it,* she thought. *I can't pretend I forgive her.* "Good. Keep it up."

The hurt on Miss Calendar's face made Buffy feel ashamed. So did her words. "Don't worry. I will."

"Uh, wait. Um . . ." She pulled it together. And she said something that was true. Gazing steadily at the Gypsy, she said, "He misses you. He doesn't say anything to me, but I know he does. I don't want him to be lonely." She paused. "I don't want anyone to."

It was a moment. Their moment. Miss Calendar softened, relaxed. "Buffy, you know that if I have a chance to make this up—"

"We're good here." *As long as it's not about her and me, I can deal.* "Let's just leave it."

Giles was talking about some flyers with a couple of students. "Yes, so, could you hang those up? Thanks so much." He brightened as Buffy approached.

"Buffy, so how was your night?"

"Sleepless," she said honestly. "But no human fatalities."

"I found a ritual to revoke the invitation to vampires," he announced.

Cordelia stepped up with total relief. "Oh, thank goodness. I actually had to talk my grandmother into switching cars with me last night."

Giles blinked in astonishment at Cordelia, then continued on with his explanation. "The ritual is fairly basic, actually. It's just the recitation of a few simple rhyming couplets, burning of moss herbs, sprinkling of holy water—"

"All stuff I have in my house," Buffy drawled.

"Hanging of cross . . ." Giles went on.

They walked.

Do they count if you hide them? Willow wondered, as she finished nailing a crucifix in place and covering it with her plaid bedroom curtains.

She said to Buffy and Cordelia, "I'm going to have a hard time explaining this to my dad."

Buffy frowned slightly. "You really think it'll bother him?"

"Ira Rosenberg's only daughter nailing crucifixes to her bedroom wall?" Willow nodded with weary affection. "I have to go over to Xander's house just to watch 'A Charlie Brown Christmas' every year."

Buffy grimaced. "I see your point."

"Although it is worthwhile to see him do the Snoopy dance," Willow allowed, this time with affection but no weariness.

Cordelia, who was wandering around Willow's room,

piped up. "Willow, are you aware that there are no fish in your aquarium?"

Willow whimpered. Buffy stepped in.

"You know, Cordelia," she said, "we've already done your car. Call it a night if you want."

"Right. Thanks. And you know I'd do the same for you if you *had* a social life." She picked up her coat from Willow's bed. There was an envelope beside it.

A brown parchment envelope.

"Oh." She picked it up and handed it to Willow. "This must be for you."

Willow and Buffy exchanged looks. Nervously, Willow opened the flap and pulled out the by now familiar stationery. She opened it. She tensed and looked hard at Buffy. "It's for you," she said meaningfully.

Buffy opened it. It was another sketch by Angelus, this one a perfect likeness of her mother, asleep. *Or not asleep . . .*

"Mom," Buffy blurted.

Angelus was waiting at the side of the driveway when Buffy's mother finally drove up. She wasn't even out of the car when he approached, holding the door open through the opened window as she turned off the engine.

"Mrs. Summers," he said in a rush, pouring on the anguish, "I need to talk to you."

She was polite but wary. "You're . . . Angel."

He beamed, shutting the door for her. She was carrying a bag of groceries, which he did not offer to carry. It would slow her down, just a little, if she needed slowing down.

"Did Buffy tell you about us?"

"She told me she wants you to leave her alone." Her voice was firm, her look steady. *A good mom. How nice.*

"I can't," he said, smiling. "I can't do that."

Joyce did not smile back. "You're scaring her."

"You have to help me," he said in a rush. She brushed past him and he whirled around to keep up with her. "Joyce, I need to be with her. You can convince her. You have to convince her." He talked fast, aiming for slightly incoherent. *Whatever gets the job done.*

It was working. Her voice was less steady as she stopped and looked hard at him. She was getting scared.

"Look, I'm telling you to leave her alone."

He pushed harder. "You have to talk to her for me, Joyce. Tell her I need her."

"Please. I just want to get inside."

She moved around him, practically about to break into a run. Angelus had to work not to chuckle.

And then, as he caught up, he "accidentally" bumped her grocery bag. It tumbled out of her arms, oranges rolling like pool balls. "You don't understand, Joyce." He gathered up one or two. "I'll die without Buffy. She'll die without me."

She bent to retrieve her groceries, froze, and looked at him. "Are you threatening her?"

"Please, why is she doing this to me?"

Her fear was mounting. "I'm calling the police, *now.*"

She got up quickly and took the porch steps quickly. Her shaking hands fumbled with her keys; she was trying hard to get the door open, but she was too freaked to do a good job of it. Joining her on the porch, Angelus smiled as he watched her awkwardness. It was time to deliver the final blow.

"I haven't been able to sleep since the night we made love," he said sadly. Her head whipped toward him. *Gotcha.* "I need her. I know you understand."

She was stunned. Speechless for a beat. Then she got the door opened and darted inside, calling, "Just leave us alone."

Now I'll go in for the kill—

But as he tried to cross the threshold, his way was blocked by an invisible barrier. He gasped in surprise.

Buffy and Willow were walking down the stairs. Willow had a spellbook open, and she was reciting an incantation in Latin.

"His verbes, consenus rescissus est."

Buffy stared at him with pure hatred on her lovely face. "Sorry, Angel," she said. "I've changed the locks."

She slammed the door in his face.

In the darkened school computer lab, Jenny sipped her herbal tea and typed another command, her gaze glued to the screen as she waited to see what happened next. She was startled when Giles appeared in the doorway with a gentle, "Hello."

"Oh, hi." She cleared the screen as she smiled at him.

He ventured into the room. "You're working late."

"Special project," she tossed off, crossing her legs, so very pleased to see him. She added softly, "I spoke to Buffy today."

That clearly pleased him. He came up to her and sat on the corner of her desk. "Yes?"

She picked up a pencil for something to do, and murmured coyly, "She said you missed me."

"Well . . . she's a meddlesome girl." Which, for Giles, was as much as admitting that it was true.

"Rupert," she began, and he looked at her. *It's not time to be sidetracked,* she reminded herself. "Okay, I don't want to say anything if I'm wrong, but I may have some news. Now I need to finish up here." She gestured to her keyboard. Then she called up her courage and asked, "Can I see you later?"

"Yes, yes," he said. He gazed at her. "You could stop by my house."

Her smile was mildly flirtatious. "Okay."

"Good." He broke into a wide grin, ducked his head, and took his leave. In the doorway, he turned back to look at her once last time.

Jenny smiled after him, and went back to her work.

The proprietor of the Dragon's Cove magic store had just turned off the neon Open sign when someone came in through the door.

Damn, he thought, barely glancing at his female prospective customer as he blew out some of the burning candles. "Sorry, honey. We're closed."

Then he turned and really looked at the vampire who stood in the glare of the streetlights with a wriggling white dog in her grasp.

She glided into the store. He thought he was going to wet his pants.

He stammered, "Wh-what do *you* want?"

"Miss Sunshine here tells me you had a visitor today," she said pleasantly, quietly. Staring off into space, she added, "But she worries." And then she turned her full attention on him, and his blood ran cold. "She wants to know what you and the mean teacher talked about."

He knew in that moment that one way or another, he would tell her.

Like any good computer person, Jenny lost track of time as she continued working on translating the annals for the Rituals of the Undead. She sat in the darkened room, oblivious to everything except her keyboard and her screen. As she hit Select All and pressed Save As, she fiddled anxiously with a pencil and talked to the screen.

"Come on, come on," she murmured.

The right-hand side of screen began filling up with new text. She skimmed it and, in that moment, she knew she had it. "That's it!" She allowed herself a joyful laugh as she copied her achievement onto a diskette. "It's going to work. This will work."

Can I code or not? she thought happily, as she started a printout. She rolled on her chair over to the old-fashioned tractor-feed printer and watched the characters printing.

Then she raised her line of sight just slightly and jumped up in sheer fright.

Angelus sat at a desk with a smile on his face, watching her.

"Angel." She struggled not to panic as she slowly backed away. *I'll just get to the door,* she told herself. *I'll make it to the door.* "How did you get in here?"

"I was invited," he said innocently, shrugging as if it were obvious. "The sign in front of the school? *Formatia trans sicere educatorum.*"

Jenny said breathlessly, " 'Enter, all ye who seek knowledge.' "

He chuckled and got to his feet. "What can I say? I'm a knowledge seeker." Holding out his hands, he started walking toward her.

Her panic level rose, but she kept herself composed. "Angel," she tried, "I've got good news."

"I heard." He sounded as if he were speaking to a child. "You went shopping at the local boogedy-boogedy store."

The glow on her desk attracted him. He picked up the crystal sphere and his voice dropped. "The orb of Thesulah. If memory serves, this is supposed to summon a person's soul from the ether, store it until it can be transferred."

He held it up. "You know what I hate most about these things?" he asked pleasantly. Then he hurled it against the blackboard, shattering it dangerously close to her head. Jenny ducked and screamed.

He laughed. "They're so damned fragile. Must be that shoddy Gypsy craftsmanship, huh?"

She made herself move, made herself glance over her shoulder, in search of the doorknob. *Oh, God, he's going to kill me,* she thought. Then, *I can't panic. I cannot.*

He turned his attention to her computer. "I never cease

to be amazed how much the world has changed in just two and a half centuries."

She reached the doorknob. It was all she could do to keep from screaming.

The door was locked.

"It's a miracle to me," he told her, wide-eyed. You put the secret to restoring my soul in here . . ." Savagely, he flung the computer to the floor. The monitor smashed against the linoleum and burst into flames. "And it comes out here." He ripped the printout off the printer. "The Ritual of Restoration. Wow." He chuckled. "This brings back memories."

He tore it in half.

"Wait! That's your—"

"Oh. My 'cure'?" He grimaced an apology as he kept ripping. "No thanks. Been there, done that. And déjà vu just isn't what it used to be.

"Well, isn't this my lucky day." He held the pages over the burning monitor. "The computer *and* the pages." He set them on fire and dropped them. Then he crouched low over the flames and made a show of warming his hands. "Looks like I get to kill two birds with one stone."

Her heart was thundering. She was so terrified she was almost blind. *Go, go,* she told herself, and she started edging toward the next door, which was parallel with Angel. But then he turned to her, in full vamp face, and drawled, "And teacher makes three."

I have to make a run for it now, she thought, racing for the door. He sprang up and caught her easily, and she screamed. With the supernatural strength of his kind, he flung her toward the wall. With bone-crunching force, she hit the door, and slid down it even as the momentum of the impact pushed it open.

She was momentarily dazed, but the adrenaline in her system propelled her on. Slowly, he advanced. Her forehead bleeding, she got to her feet, panting with fear, and flew down the corridor.

"Oh, good," Angelus said dangerously. "I need to work up an appetite first."

She raced for her life, her heels clattering as she reached the first set of swinging doors in the corridor. Then she ran to the right, past the lockers, and to the exit.

The door was locked.

She doubled back and saw his shadow looming through the panels of glass in the double doors. She took another exit. Down the breezeway she ran, arms pumping, looking back to see him shortening the distance between them. Light and shadow played on his monstrous features.

Like a quarry run to ground, she was forced to another entrance into the school. For a few horrible moments, she thought that door was locked too, but it finally gave way under her frantic pushes.

She lost time and he was practically on top of her by the time she got the door open. He growled like an animal, anticipating the kill. She slammed the door in his face and ran on.

The bright overhead fluorescents cast an eerie, cold blue glow over the two of them as she lost more ground. Then she saw the janitor's cleaning cart and pushed it at him. It slammed into him and he was flung over it, landing hard on the floor.

While he was down, she took the nearby flight of stairs. On the landing, gasping for breath, she looked over her shoulder as she darted past a semicircular window—streetlamps and passing cars, the unsuspecting and uncaring normal world of suburban night—and ran right into him.

How? she thought, but then all other thoughts fled. Her eyes widened as he put his chilled fingers to her lips, urging her to silence. His laughter was inhuman. She couldn't breathe. Couldn't blink. Couldn't breathe.

Rupert—

"Sorry, Jenny. This is where you get off," he said in a low, gentle voice. And then he grabbed her head and twisted.

Her neck made an interesting crack.

Her lovely body tumbled to the floor.

A little winded, Angelus took a couple of deep breaths, and then he cocked his head.

Invigorated, he said, "I never get tired of doing that."

Without another glance at the dead woman, he moved on.

CHAPTER 3

There was a chipper rap on the Summers' door, and Willow quickly answered it. It was Giles.

"Willow," he said with brisk British pleasantness. "Good evening."

"Hi. Come on in." She was cheery because she had just seen firsthand that the ritual worked. *Angelus can't hurt any of us anymore.* "Here's the book." She held out the volume that contained the de-invitation ritual.

"Right. I guess I should do my apartment tonight." He glanced down at the book, then up at Willow. "Did the ritual go all right?"

"Oh, yeah. It went fine." She made a little face. "Well, it went fine until the part where Angel showed up and told Buffy's mom that he and Buffy had . . ." She trailed off and looked away, a bit embarrassed. She tried again.

163

"Well, you know, that they had . . . you know." She still couldn't come right out and say it.

And then she thought, *Uh-oh, did I just spill the beans?* She asked hopefully, "You *do* know, right?"

He blinked and said, "Oh, yes, sorry."

"Oh, good." She heaved a sigh of relief. Then she went on to explain, "Because I just realized that being a librarian and all, you maybe didn't know."

He seemed just the tiniest smidgen indignant. "No. Thank you. I got it."

"You would have been proud of her, though. She totally kept her cool," she informed him. There was a silence. She moved her shoulders and smiled. "Okay. Well, I'll tell Buffy you stopped by."

He glanced up at the ceiling, gesturing in the direction of the stairs and said, "Do you think perhaps I should intervene on Buffy's behalf with her mother? Maybe, say something?"

How nice, Willow thought. "Sure. Like what would you say?" she asked helpfully.

He mumbled around for a few seconds. Willow realized he was stuck, so she opened the door to give him a graceful exit. For which he appeared grateful.

"You will tell Buffy I dropped by?" He sailed through the door.

"You bet," she assured him, and shut the door.

The tension in the room was thick and jumpy. Buffy sat on her bed while her mother paced.

"That stuff with the Latin and the herbs, he's just real superstitious."

"Oh." Looking thoroughly unconvinced, and disappointed that Buffy would even say such a thing, much less believe it, Joyce crossed her arms and slowly sat on Buffy's vanity bench.

So Buffy tried again. "We just thought if—"

Joyce put her hands on her knees and took a deep breath. "Was he the first? No. Wait." She got to her feet and paced again. "I don't want to know. I don't *think* I want to."

"Yes," Buffy said heavily. *There's too much here to explain. It's so much more than what other girls have to talk about . . .* "He was the first. I mean, the only."

"He's older than you."

Buffy was too upset to laugh at the irony. "I know."

"*Too* old, Buffy. And he's obviously not very stable. I really wish . . . I just thought you would show more judgment."

It hurt badly not to be able to defend herself. To explain what they had gone through. Almost dying. Knowing that the world might soon be over.

"He wasn't like this before." *He wasn't a demon. He wasn't evil.*

"Are you in love with him?"

"I was."

"Were you careful?"

Buffy reeled. That was so much a question for another kind of life. *Not my kind.* "Mom, this is no time—"

"Don't 'Mom' me, Buffy," her mother said sharply. "You don't get to get out of this. You had sex with a boy you didn't even see fit to tell me you were dating."

Almost by rote, Buffy said flatly. "I made a mistake."

"Well, don't say that just to shut me up because I think you really did."

"I know that." She was about to burst with the unfairness of it. "I can't tell you *everything*."

"How about *anything?*" Joyce said, frustrated. "Buffy, you can shut me out of your life. I am pretty much used to that. But don't expect me to stop caring about you because it's never going to happen. I love you more than anything in the world."

She took a breath and sat down next to Buffy. In a sad, uncertain voice, she said, "That would be your cue to roll your eyes and tell me I'm grossing you out."

Buffy's eyes were welling. *Mom, I'm so sorry. I wish I could tell you. I so need to tell you.*

Quietly, she murmured, "You're not."

They both struggled for a moment. Then Joyce lifted her head slightly and said, "Oh, well." She considered. "I guess that was the talk."

Buffy took that in. "So how'd it go?"

"I don't know." Her mother smiled faintly at her. "It was my first."

There was a long-stemmed red rose angled between the knob and the jamb of Giles's front door. The corners of his mouth twitched slightly.

She's here, he thought, warming with anticipation.

He lifted the rose and inhaled its lovely scent, his smile growing. Then he opened the door, poking in his head and called, "Hello?" He shut the door and set down his briefcase. "Jenny? It's me."

To the passionate strains of Puccini's *La Boheme*, he took off his coat. That was when he saw the bottle of wine cooling in the bucket and the note on parchment paper.

Upstairs, it read. He smiled, a bit flustered, and looked upward, in the direction of his loft bed. He put down the envelope and took off his glasses. Smoothed back his hair. He felt years younger, lighter; he felt himself to be a man quite in love with a beautiful young woman, who wanted him.

Unable to give voice to the emotion rising within him, he let the soaring opera music do it for him.

He took up the wine and the two glasses that were beside the bucket. On each step which led to his beloved, a votive candle glowed. The stairs were strewn with roses. Softly, he ascended, as the opera duet crescendoed, the full, throaty voices rising in desperate yearning.

There she is. She was lying on his bed, her dark hair piled on the pillows like a filigreed frame, her exquisite features a study in heart-stopping beauty.

His heart rose; he felt the glow of the candles in his skin. So beautiful, lying so still . . .

So still . . .

Her eyes, staring, as if she were . . .

As if . . .

The wine bottle crashed to the floor.

So still, Giles stood against the wall. His eyes staring, as if he were dead.

The blue and red lights of the police cars flashed

across the walls of his apartment; the dispatcher's crack-ling voice buzzed crazily, like a hornet.

He did not look as a police officer and a man in a blue jumpsuit marked Coroner wheeled the loaded body bag past him.

Then the officer in charge said, not without compas-sion, "Mr. Giles, we're going to have to ask you to come with us. Just to answer a few questions."

It was then that he felt a flicker of what might pass for life. Rousing himself as best he could, he mur-mured. "Of course. Yes. Procedure." Giles looked at him. "I need to make a phone call, if that's all right."

Through the window that looked into the Slayer's din-ing room, Angelus watched.

The Slayer was walking with Willow through the room. Willow asked, "So, was it horrible?"

"It wasn't too horrible," the Slayer replied.

Passion is the source of our finest moments, Angelus thought. *The joy of love, the clarity of hatred, and the ecstasy of grief.*

The phone rang. The Slayer ran back through the din-ing room to grab it. Upbeat, she lifted the receiver and put it to her ear. Her lips moved to say, "Hello? Giles." She leaned against the wood and plaster wall. "Hey, we finished the sp—"

And then, as she listened, she went slack. Angelus bent eagerly, observing each shattering moment as she limply handed the phone to Willow.

Which is more fulfilling? the vampire pondered. *The utter shock of the Slayer as she slides to the floor or the frightened, grief-stricken weeping of her little redheaded companion?*

Summoned by the sobbing, Joyce Summers ran into the room, embracing Willow as Buffy buried her head against her knees.

With a smile, Angelus faded into the night.

It's all so perfect. It couldn't be better.

My work here is done.

While Willow and Buffy waited numbly at the curb outside the Summers' house, Cordelia and Xander finally pulled up in Cordelia's garlic-and-cross-laden car.

"Where's Giles?" Buffy asked as soon as Xander got out.

Xander said, "No luck. By the time we got to the station, the cops said he'd already left. I guess they just wanted to ask him some questions."

Buffy looked down, frowning. Then she said, "Cordelia, will you drive us to Giles's house?"

Cordelia inclined her head. "Of course."

Willow looked at Buffy. "But do you think maybe he wants to be alone?"

Buffy gazed back at her. "I'm not worried about what he wants. I'm worried about what he's going to do."

They climbed into the car.

Giles's wooden weapons chest was open. He drew a sword and tested its strength and sharpness. He decided against it. Then he loaded the gas can on top of an open sling bag crammed with weapons, from a crossbow to a mace to an old dueling pistol to wooden stakes.

His eyes were filled with icy rage. His face was stony, impassive.

He picked up the bag and left.

On his desk, a brown parchment drawing lay in the diffuse light of an Arts and Crafts lamp: Jenny, her head lying on Giles's pillow, her eyes open.

In death.

CHAPTER 4

There was yellow police tape across the door. Buffy stood just behind Xander as he opened the door and called steadily, "Hello? Giles?"

He ducked under the tape. Willow followed, then Cordelia, and last, Buffy. Xander noted the wine bucket. "I guess Giles had a big night planned tonight."

Buffy picked up the sketch of Jenny Calendar. "Giles didn't set this up. Angel did. This is the wrapping for the gift." She handed the sketch to Xander.

He shut his eyes as Buffy moved past him and headed up the stairs. "Oh, man. Poor Giles."

Willow walked over to the empty weapons chest. "Look. All his weapons are gone."

Cordelia came up beside her and glanced inside as well. "But I thought he kept his weapons at the library?"

"No. Those are his everyday weapons." Xander looked up from the sketch. "These were his 'good' weapons. The ones he breaks out when company comes to visit."

Buffy came down the stairs and paused on the landing.

Willow said, "So he's not here?"

"Well, then, where is he?" Cordelia asked.

"He'll go to wherever Angel is," Buffy said flatly.

Willow looked at Buffy. "That means the factory, right?"

"So Giles is going to try to kill Angel, then," Cordelia said.

Xander's voice was acid and bitter. "Well, it's about time somebody did."

"*Xander*," Willow said, shocked.

"I'm sorry. But let's not forget that I hated Angel long before you guys jumped on the bandwagon. So I think I deserve something for not saying 'I told you so' long before now. And if Giles wants to go after the fiend," he turned to Buffy, as if he wanted to make sure she heard him use the word, "that murdered his girlfriend, I say, 'Faster, pussycat. Kill. Kill.' "

Buffy said simply, "You're right."

Xander did not take the moment to garner credit. His voice was low and calm as he said, "Thank you."

Buffy came the rest of the way down the stairs. "There's only one thing wrong with Giles's little revenge scenario."

"And what's that?" Xander asked, in a slightly challenging tone.

Buffy's face clouded with worry.

"It's going to get him killed."

Angelus was loving the look of disbelief and anger on Spike's face.

"Are you insane? We're supposed to kill the girl, not leave gag gifts in her friends' beds."

With Sunshine under her arm, Dru leapt to Angelus's defense. Carefully, diplomatically, she said, "But, Spike, the bad teacher was going to restore Angel's soul."

"What if she did?" Spike shrugged. "If you ask me, I find myself preferring the old, Buffy-whipped Angelus. Because this new improved one is not playing with a full sack."

Spike pressed on, staring at Angelus while he spoke to Dru. "Hey, I love a good slaughter as much as the next bloke, but his little pranks will only leave us with one incredibly brassed-off Slayer."

"Don't worry, Roller Boy," Angelus bit off. He folded his arms across his chest. "I've got everything under control."

Almost before the words were out of his mouth, a Molotov cocktail hit the table and burst into roaring flame. Angelus and Dru ran past the table and the wooden high-back chairs, Spike wheeling up behind.

As they fled, an arrow pierced Angelus's shoulder. Gritting his teeth from the pain, he stopped to pull it out. He looked up to see Rupert Giles advancing calmly on him, a baseball bat in his hand. The human dipped the bat into the fire and kept advancing. Before Angelus had time to defend himself, the Watcher hit him square in the face with the flaming bat, then backhanded him the other way.

"Geez, whatever happened to wooden stakes?" Angelus got out, grimacing as he hunched over in pain. Giles slammed the bat down on him yet again.

Dru bolted forward to help, but Spike wrapped his hand around her forearm and said, "Ah-ahhh. No fair going into the ring unless he tags you first."

The Watcher got off a half-dozen more blows before Angelus got up to his feet, rose to his full height, and blocked the downward arc of the bat. He grabbed Giles by the throat and dangled him above the floor. The baseball bat clattered to the floor as Giles lost consciousness.

"All right, you've had your fun," Angelus raged. "But you know what it's time for now?"

Suddenly he was pulled away and thrown backward. Then, as Buffy kicked him brutally in the jaw, she shouted, "*My* fun."

Though their movements were masked by spreading fire, Angelus was aware that Dru and Spike were making their escape as the Slayer threw him to his knees. She got in one more strong kick before he recovered and flung her over his shoulder. While she steadied herself, he ran up the stairs. Grabbing a metal reinforcing rod, she tripped him and he began to slide back down the stairs.

He kicked her and she fell backward. He got up the stairs and headed for the gangway. But she jumped up some wooden crates and met him on the catwalk.

The fire was growing below them as he swung at her.

Flames glowed on the walls. She dodged and clipped him behind his knee. He grunted and collapsed, and while he was down, she looped a rope around his neck and slammed him from side to side, battering him mercilessly. Then she slammed her foot into his midsection and rammed him backward. As he got to his feet, she leaped up, held on to a pipe, and kicked him in the chest again.

He staggered and fell, taking barrels and pipes with him. The flames rose up, adding an interesting new dimension to their battle. She was most definitely gaining the upper hand.

He charged her again and she threw him down again, and started whaling on him.

Didn't I remind Spike she's the strongest Slayer we've ever faced? he thought. *She's going to kill me if I don't get away from her.*

But she hasn't been paying attention to the fire.

He laughed as if it were all a big game and said, "Are you going to let your old man just burn?"

Buffy ticked her glance from Angel to the bottom level of the burning factory. The flames were rushing toward Giles, who lay unconscious on the floor.

Oh, no, she thought. The decision was too horrible, too unfair: Angelus's life for Giles's. If she didn't drag Giles out of the way, he would surely die.

If she didn't kill Angelus now, she might never get another chance. And more people would definitely die. He had already threatened everyone she loved. And keep-out spells in houses were not enough. Any time any of them went outside in the dark, he might attack. Buffy couldn't be everywhere, protecting everybody. *Sooner or later, he'll kill someone.*

But Giles is going to die now, if I don't save him . . .

Angelus took advantage of her distraction to toss her over the side. She caught herself, then jumped the rest of the way down. As Angelus got away, she forced Giles to his feet and half-carried, half-dragged him out of the building.

The fresh air roused him. "Why did you come here?" he shouted at her, pushing her away. "This wasn't your fight!"

Her answer was a solid roundhouse to his jaw. He collapsed facedown on the ground. "Are you trying to get yourself killed?" she screamed at him.

The hard tears came. She fell down beside him, clinging to him as they both wept. He shook with his grief and rage; she with her desperation, hopelessness, and fear.

And sorrow for him.

Her very deep sorrow.

"You can't leave me." It was a plea. "I can't do this alone."

Together, they wept.

Much later, Giles slowly climbed the steps to his apartment. He paused at the door, and pulled away the yellow police tape.

Angelus watched, and thought, *It hurts sometimes, more than we can bear. If we could live without passion, maybe we'd know some kind of peace. But we would be hollow . . . empty rooms . . . shuttered and dank. Without passion, we'd be truly dead.*

It was a cold, gray day. In the cemetery, leaves floated on a small pond of gray water not far from Jenny Calendar's gravestone. Leaves had fluttered down on it as well, like the butterfly kisses Giles had once dreamed of brushing against her temples and cheeks.

He knelt on one knee, as one might when proposing marriage, and laid roses on the rectangle of sod newly draped over the freshly dug grave. For a moment, he stayed there, and there was something noble in his grief. Something strong.

It communicated itself to Buffy.

He rose and put his hand in the pocket of his raincoat. "In my years as Watcher, I've buried too many people. Jenny was the first one I loved."

Beside him, in her gray raincoat and boots, Buffy said with all her heart, "I'm sorry. I'm sorry I couldn't kill him for you . . . for her . . . when I had the chance."

They both looked down at the simple headstone. *Jennifer Calendar,* was all it said. Nothing of Janna. Nothing of curses and betrayals.

Nothing of passion.

"I wasn't ready," Buffy admitted, "but I think I finally am."

Miss Calendar's computer science students were utterly silent when Willow walked in, her notebook and text in her arms. She said, a bit shyly, "Hi. Principal Snyder has asked me to fill in for Miss Calendar until the new computer science teacher arrives. So I'm just going to stick to the lesson plan she left."

She walked around the desk and put down her things.

At the gravesite, Buffy said to Giles, "I can't hold on to the past any more. Angel is gone. Nothing's ever going to bring him back."

And in Willow's computer science classroom, she unknowingly knocked a yellow diskette off the desk. Sliding between the desk and the portable storage cart Miss Calendar had drawn up beside it, the disk clattered to the floor.

It rested there, at an angle.

Waiting.

THE CHRONICLES:
EPILOGUE

Hands in the pockets of his black duster, Angelus studied the darkened window of the Slayer's bedroom on the second floor of the house on Revello Drive. The moon glowed on his pale face and made hollows in his cheeks and around his eyes.

"Buffy," he whispered. "I will taunt and torment you. I will spend my nights hounding you. I will make your life a living hell, and you'll wish I had killed you to put you out of your misery."

In the dark night, he smiled, wondering if she was actually able to sleep any more. If her fear and anger kept her up nights. Her eyes open, staring into the dark, her heart thudding thickly. Tears building, spilling. Because of him.

His mind swam with vivid, detailed images of the Chosen One. Buffy, smiling at him. Buffy, weeping.

Buffy.

I will break her, he thought, clenching his fists, savoring the times that were to come. Drawing out her torment. Hurting her beyond bearing, over and over again. Making sure she never stopped thinking about what he could do, what he would do, to everyone she loved.

To her.

That was far more sublime than simply snuffing out her existence. Destruction versus a quick, clean death, such as he had given Jenny Calendar.

Spike didn't understand. Spike couldn't understand. What did a weakling like Roller Boy know about hatred?

About passion?

Angelus stared at the window. He stood there for hours, until the sun threatened him.

Even then, he almost stayed, seething, unable to stop staring at the window of her bedroom.

That's how much I hate her—

With a passion.

That's what he told himself, as he whirled on his heel and vanished into the darkness.

ABOUT THE AUTHOR

Four-time Bram Stoker Award winner Nancy Holder has sold forty novels and over two hundred short stories, articles, and essays. Her work has appeared on the *Los Angeles Times, USA Today,* and Amazon.com bestseller lists. Alone and with her frequent collaborator, Christopher Golden, she has written a dozen *Buffy the Vampire Slayer* projects, including *The Watcher's Guide* and *Immortal,* the first *Buffy* hardcover novel, due out for Halloween 1999. She has also written several short stories with Golden, and appears in two of the anthologies he edited, including the award-winning *CUT!: Horror Writers on Horror Film.*

Holder's work has been translated into two dozen languages, and she has also written comic books, game fiction, and television commercials. She is currently completing the last volume of a science fiction trilogy called *Gambler's Star* for Avon Books.

A graduate of the University of California at San Diego, she lives in San Diego with her husband, Wayne, and their daughter, Belle.

Buffy: "Willow, why don't you compile a list of kids who've died here who might have turned into ghosts."

Xander: "We're on a Hellmouth. It's gonna be a long list."

Willow: "Have you seen the 'In Memorium' section in the yearbook?"

BUFFY

THE VAMPIRE

SLAYER™

How *does* the Sunnydale yearbook staff memorialize all the less fortunate classmates?

Get your very own copy of the Slayer's Sunnydale High School yearbook, full of cast photos, school event wrap-ups, and personal notes from Buffy's best buds.

THE SUNNYDALE HIGH YEARBOOK

By Christopher Golden and Nancy Holder

Available Fall 1999

Published by Pocket Books

BODY OF EVIDENCE THRILLERS
Starring Jenna Blake

"The first day at college, my professor dropped dead. The second day, I assisted at his autopsy. Let's hope I don't have to go through four years of this...."

When Jenna Blake starts her freshman year at Somerset University, it's an exciting time, filled with new faces and new challenges, not to mention parties and guys and...a job interview with the medical examiner that takes place in the middle of an autopsy! As Jenna starts her new job, she is drawn into a web of dangerous politics and deadly disease...a web that will bring her face to face with a pair of killers: one medical, and one all too human.

Body Bags
Thief of Hearts
Soul Survivor
(Available November 1999)

By Christopher Golden
Bestselling coauthor of
Buffy the Vampire Slayer™ _The Watcher's Guide_

Published by Pocket Pulse Books